HUMAN WARMTH & OTHER STORIES

Daniel Curzon

HUMAN WARMTH
&
OTHER STORIES

Grey Fox Press
San Francisco

Some of the stories included here were first published in *Blueboy, Christopher Street, Gay Sunshine, G.P.U. News,* and *Kansas Quarterly.*

Library of Congress Cataloging in Publication Data

Curzon, Daniel.
  Human warmth & other stories.

  1. Homosexuality, Male—Fiction. I. Title.
PS3553.U73H8   813'.54   80-23270
ISBN 0-912516-54-2 (pbk.)

Distributed by The Subterranean Company,
  P.O. Box 10233, Eugene, Oregon 97440.

To H. W. S.
for all your support

contents

preface

It seems to me there are two types of gay fiction. One emphasizes the particular events of gay life, such as coming out of the closet. The second type emphasizes realities that could happen to anyone, such as being afraid of dying. Both types, I believe, are worthwhile. Nongay readers, no doubt, can relate most to fiction that isn't completely foreign to their own experience, but the real breath of fresh air of the gay literary movement surely is that we're writing about what has never been written about before in the history of the world. Even Greek literature doesn't deal with what I've lived.

I think my short stories fall into those two categories, with some overlap. I think anybody can read them. The question that annoys me, as a writer, the most is: "When are you going to write something that isn't gay?" Answer: It's the taboo that's the problem, not the subject matter. But some people, even gays, think homosexual themes are too specialized. Yet they're no more specialized than stories about the South or Russia. I'm a "gay writer" in the same way that Flannery O'Connor is a "Southern writer," that is, not *just* a Southern writer. In other words, I hope that all my stories last and are read centuries from now, but most literature dates and comes to be read for historical interest more than for anything else. I've tried to achieve some kind of universality even when dealing with very specific homosexual content, but only time can tell if I've succeeded, I guess.

In general I've included more touching, more compassionate stories in this collection than in my first book of stories, *The Revolt of the Perverts*. Sometimes I think I'm not being an honest writer if I don't make my characters selfish, venal, and cruel, but then again, I like to read stories that engage my tenderer feelings, and maybe other people do too. (I *know* other people do too.)

Enjoy this book. Art is better than the life that feeds it.

Daniel Curzon

HUMAN WARMTH & OTHER STORIES

the housewife and the homosexual

HER VIEW

"Spit that out!" she demanded, leaving the pram for a moment in order to grab him by the shoulder and squeeze on his jaws. "Spit that out!" After another moment of resistance, Neville discharged the chewed chips into her hand. She took out the paper toweling from the big purse she carried for just such emergencies, then stuffed the wrapped bits into the purse because there was no litter barrel in sight. "Dirty!" she reprimanded, pointing at the cement of the pier, where he'd picked up the chips. "You'll get sick if you eat dirty things!" She turned back to Jamie, who'd started to rip one of the grocery bags Barbara had placed at his back. Two cans of Tesco peas fell out and landed on the baby's leg. Jamie began to cry, and Barbara leaned down and lifted him against her chest, crooning. "It doesn't hurt; it doesn't hurt. There, there!" The tiny mouth spilled open, not persuaded, and the white circle of baby teeth and red, sore gums struggled for breath. She kissed the spot on the child's leg and walked back and forth, pressing Jamie to her breasts to comfort him.

Meanwhile, Neville had forgotten the chips and was pushing the pram down the pier away from Barbara and his baby brother. But at three he wasn't strong enough to guide it. "Mind the edge!" she called, rushing toward the boy. "Mind the edge!" Her red-cheeked face went pale with apprehension.

A slender man in his early twenties spotted the potential disaster, set down his overnight bag, and caught hold of the pram.

Barbara was there in a second. "Oh, thank you! Thank you!" she said to the slim young man, who was attractive, with hot blue eyes, a suntan she knew he couldn't have gotten in England, and an open shirt that revealed the dark hairs at the base of his throat. "How can I ever thank you!" she said, taking Neville's hand out of the young man's.

"Don't worry about it." If there was a flaw in the young man, she noticed, it was that he didn't quite stand up straight—a bit round-shouldered. She looked down at Neville, whom she knew was going to grow up to be a handsome man too. *I'll have to keep after him to stand up straight!*

"Can I help?" the young man offered, seeing that Barbara had one child in the crook of one arm and the older boy by the hand.

"If you could just push the pram away from the edge," she replied, smiling her relief. To Neville she said, "Oh, aren't you awful! Don't you push this pram ever again, you little demon!" She gave his wrist a severe, but loving, shake.

Neville looked momentarily shamefaced, but was distracted by the sight of the ferry coming into Portsmouth Harbor.

"You stay right here by me!" she warned when she saw he was about to run after the other passengers at the entranceway. She put the baby back into the pram and fastened the strap of the restraining harness, then tucked the peas behind a pillow. She shook her finger hard. "Don't you dare touch that carrier bag again, Jamie!" She was thinking of the vase he'd pulled off the table in the reception room at home and broken, the Wedgwood vase her mother had given her for a wedding present.

"Why don't I push the baby carriage along for you, until you get on the boat?" the slender young man suggested.

"Oh, thank you!" She lifted Jamie into her arms again, noticing that the young man with the hot blue eyes had a pin on the lapel of his sport jacket. It said C.H.E. on it. "Are you an American?" she wondered.

"Canadian!" he answered, following her and her sons, pushing the pram full of groceries, until they stopped at the entranceway, watching the crew members tying the heavy ropes. After a moment the gangplank began to creak toward them.

"Have you been in England long?" she said. "Jamie's just learning to walk," she went on, setting the smaller child down. He tottered and held onto her skirt as she straightened her mussed yellow hair with her free hand and caught Neville's sleeve with the other. "But you—you've been walking into mischief since you were ten months old, haven't you!" she said teasingly to the older boy.

"They keep you busy!" the young man said, nodding his head of brunet hair (almost the color of dark grapes) at the children.

"I couldn't begin to tell you!" she said with mock weariness. "Neville was three yesterday, and he never stops for a minute! We had a little accident in the toilet at lunch time, didn't we, Neville!" She gave the boy an affectionate look, quite happy to tell this stranger about her troubles, the clean, red color returned to her face, a full face that was twenty-five years old but could have been a few years older. "We came to Portsmouth for a belated birthday treat, didn't we, Neville?"

"Look, Mummy!" he answered, not concerned, much more interested in the wide gangplank that was being lowered.

"What part of Canada are you from?" she asked.

"Toronto."

"My, I've always wanted to see Toronto! But Portsmouth or Southsea are about as far as we ever get!" she said merrily. As Barbara looked around at the young man pushing her pram, she noticed the button on his lapel again and wanted to ask what it meant, but didn't think she should.

"I've never been to the Isle of Wight before," the young man volunteered. "In fact, this is my first trip to Europe."

"Not too many tourists come down here—Canadians and Americans, I mean. Mostly British. Jamie!" The baby, his diaper hanging out of his playsuit, was squatting down trying to pick up some dog excrement. "Dirty! Dirty! Isn't he something!"

The young man nodded. "Someone invited me to come and stay with him for a couple of days. He owns a restaurant."

"Oh? What restaurant is it?"

"The Monks' Bay."

"Oh, it's lovely there! Mervyn and I went there for dinner once. Lovely food. Just lovely."

"That sounds good. He said I'd have a good time."

"My name's Barbara Nestley." She offered to shake hands. "And these are my sons—Jamie and Neville."

The young man bowed at all three, taking Barbara's fingers. "How do you do! I'm Jay Travert." The gangplank fell with a robust clank onto the pier.

"I couldn't help but notice your button," she said. "Do you mind if I ask what C.H.E. stands for?"

He patted the bright button. "Not at all. The Campaign for Homosexual Equality."

She leaned forward. "The Campaign for what?" she asked, afraid she hadn't heard correctly.

"It's a gay organization in England. Since I'm Canadian, I don't really belong, but I thought I'd wear it for the week or so I'm here."

Barbara was struck a little numb, looking down to see if Neville had heard the word "homosexual," but he was busy watching the crew roughhousing as they left the gangplank. Was this attractive young man admitting out loud that he was a homosexual? "Oh," she said, unable to think of an appropriate reply at first. "Do you mind if I ask why you wear a button about it?" *How sad!* she thought. *How sad and strange!*

"So the subject will come up. I think it's about time the taboo died."

"Yes, I see." She knew she was silly in being so stiff, in looking nervously at his suntanned knuckles gripped around the push-bar of her pram. But this was the first homosexual she'd ever encountered in person. "Well . . . yes . . . I didn't know they were wearing buttons."

"Only some of us," he grinned.

"Oh, I see," she said even more stiffly. "How interesting." *How very strange of them to be wearing buttons!*

"I hope the regatta at Cowes will be just as interesting. I love sailing, but I'll just be a spectator, I'm afraid."

"Are the homosexuals entering a boat this year?"

"No, not as such, I don't believe."

"Yes, that should be lovely this year. The weather has been remarkably warm." Barbara peered at the young man's attractive face again, inspecting it for . . . for she didn't know quite what. He looked quite normal. *Of course that article in the women's magazine said most of them do look quite normal, but somehow I never expected this young man to be one of them. Not that I have anything against them in the least. Mervyn condemns the queers and the poufs sometimes, but that's mostly when he's angry with his clerks. Of course they can't help themselves or I suppose they would. It's just so odd him saying that he's one of them—right out loud like that!*

She didn't say any more while they were walking up the gangplank onto the ferry. "Mind your step, Neville!" she said when the boy stumbled. She looked back to see that the young man was pushing the pram all right. *What will Mervyn say when I tell him I met a homosexual today!* she thought, savoring the possibilities. What would the other passengers think if they knew that the man pushing her pram wasn't her husband at all—the way it must seem—but was actually a homosexual!

"Okay?" the young man asked when they were aboard. "Care to go down into the lounge?"

"It's so lovely this afternoon, why don't we sit up on the deck?"

"Fine." He found them seats on a bench in the bow. "Is that the Isle of Wight?" He pointed. "So close?"

"It's only half an hour ride. Would you like a sweet?" Barbara held up a jam roll she'd taken from her purse.

"Why, thank you." He took it and stood near the railing, eating.

Barbara was glad the young man hadn't gone away. There were some questions—general ones, not too intimate—that she wanted to ask him, but Neville had developed the hiccups. "Hold your breath," she said. The boy, chubby in his blue sailor suit, sucked in his breath but couldn't hold it. "Hold your breath!" She pinched his nose closed while he tried again, but it was to no avail. "Well, just go on hiccuping then! I warned you not to eat so much!" She looked up at the young man for confirmation.

"They keep you busy, don't they?" the young man said, gesturing at the children.

"Never a moment's rest!" Barbara checked to see what Jamie was up to. But he was quiet, surprising her. Then she noticed that he was staring at a seagull hovering near the bowsprit. She adjusted the hood of the pram to protect Jamie's eyes from the startling sun. "Whew!" she said happily. She gave Jamie another bite of jam roll, then took one herself, wiping away the stickiness around the baby's lips.

"I want some!" Neville demanded, seeing his baby brother get the jam roll.

"You've had more than enough to eat today! You'll get sick to your stomach from the ferry and make a mess!" The little boy pouted and then hiccuped, but she didn't give in.

"This is great! the young man said, tearing off a piece of his jam roll and tossing it into the air toward the seagull near the bowsprit. The bird swooped down and picked it out of the water, which was as gray as old tea. "No more for you!" he called to the seagull.

Barbara wondered if the young man was mocking her. *He's envious of us*, she thought, feeling sorry for him. *He doesn't have a family of his own, no one to care for, no one to care for him. How empty his life must be! How can people be mean to them when they're so unlucky, so sad!* She watched him leaning on the wooden railing on his elbows. *All he has are temporary "episodes," most likely with strangers, with men he meets by accident and who invite him to their restaurants for a couple of days!* She glanced at his waist, his buttocks turned toward her. *How could anybody have sex with total strangers! How could they kiss somebody like that?* She looked again at his buttocks. *Does he really let strange men do things to him back there? Does he really? Fancy that the man who runs the Monks' Bay Restaurant is one of them! Won't Mervyn be surprised to hear that!*

"Mummy! Look!" Neville called, thrusting his forefinger at a seagull that flew right above their heads. The boy hiccuped.

"Yes, isn't it pretty!" she said.

An old couple with luggage, on the far side of the bow,

nudged each other and smiled toward her and her family. She smiled back. *Yes, Mervyn and I will travel too when the children are grown.*

The slender young man at the railing was licking his fingers. "Would you like a piece of toweling?" she asked.

"Oh, they'll dry in the wind!" he said, holding up his fingers.

How odd! Barbara thought. A sudden panic made her reach out instinctively for Neville beside her on the bench, then for Jamie, who was playing with his restraining harness. *What if Neville or Jamie became one of those! No!* Her stomach went putrid with the thought. *Oh, they mustn't! They simply mustn't! How awful for them! I'd never forgive myself! Did he grab Neville's hand because he molests little boys?* The boat moved away from the dock with a jolt.

"Have you been shopping?" the young man enquired, turning around.

"Mostly we've just had a little Awayday holiday," she answered distantly. She felt clammy and tried not to look at the young man.

"Did you get to the Chichester Festival yet?"

"Afraid we don't go." She patted Neville on the back because he still had the hiccups.

"It was excellent. They did a Turgenev. I stopped over last night."

"Mervyn's not much for plays and things like that."

"Is Mervyn your husband?"

She stood up. "Did I forget to tell you?"

"You really ought to go sometimes. Especially since it's so close."

"You're not an actor, are you?" she asked, obliquely referring to his good looks. She'd heard that many actors were . . . that way.

"Me? Never! I won't start work till this fall. I just graduated from college."

"What sort of work will it be?" She got up to turn the baby's pram so that the salty sea breeze wouldn't blow on him as they headed out into the Solent.

"As a potter."

"A what?"

"I make ceramics."

"For a living?"

He chuckled. "Yes, for a living. I have a contract with a gallery in a department store in Toronto to take my work."

"How interesting." Barbara wanted to know more and yet she also wished the young man would go away now. She spotted Neville trying to sneak off the edge of the bench. "You little demon! You stay right here! You'll fall down the steps!"

"I don't want to stay here," the little boy grumbled. He'd gotten rid of his hiccups.

"Say," the young man said as if remembering something he wanted to ask, "maybe you can tell me what I should do while I'm over on the Isle of Wight?"

"You mean for entertainment?" Barbara thought for a moment. "They have some nice Mystery Tours. You go out on a fine, big bus without knowing where they're taking you. And they bring you back by four thirty. In time for tea!" After she'd spoken, it struck her that perhaps he'd meant gay clubs or pubs. She was sure there weren't any on the island. *Could there be?*

"Maybe I'll take one of those tours then. Are they fun?"

"Oh, I haven't taken one myself. My mother did a year ago. She loved it."

"Anything else you'd recommend?"

I'm afraid I can't help you with those gay places. He has a nerve hinting, doesn't he! "We have a lovely market on Saturdays until one o'clock. You can find some real bargains there."

The young man smiled tenderly. "Well, maybe I can make that too."

Barbara felt resentful of that smile. "I don't suppose these things would appeal very much to a university graduate," she said, leaning over to see if Jamie had soiled his diaper. "Oh, I'll have to change you as soon as we land!" she said, clucking her tongue affectionately at the baby. "My little tinkler! You!"

"Perhaps I can find some unusual decanters or vases at the market. I collect them."

"Maybe you can," Barbara said in a forgiving voice. She had wanted to go to the university at Brighton very much, but she'd had no A-levels, only O-levels, in her examinations. *Well, not everybody needs all that education*, she thought. *To collect pots, no less! I can collect pots myself without going to university to learn how! Some of us have to raise children. Especially with all these selfish women on the Pill!* She looked at sweet Jamie sitting against the grocery bags. His eyes were shut as he dozed, his chubby cheeks ruddy with health. *What a darling! I might not have him if I'd gone to university. I haven't lost a thing, not a thing.*

She examined the slender young man standing nearby. He seemed shy. *I wonder if it's because I'm a woman. He's probably not used to women. The poor man! I never realized before what they must go through.* She stared up at the young man's button and asked quietly, "Have you ever tried to get a cure?"

"A cure?"

She swiveled around to be positive no one was eavesdropping. "For what you mentioned before." She pointed at the button.

He almost snorted. "But you can't get a 'cure' for what isn't an illness!" His hot blue eyes went right to her face.

"Oh, I'm sorry. I didn't mean to be insulting." Barbara was embarrassed that he'd come back at her so sharply. "But don't you get very lonely?"

"There are lots of men like me. I meet them all the time." He spread his hands, palms up.

"Well, how nice. I think people should live their own lives. Everybody should do what they want to."

The young man took a step nearer. "I must say you're being very considerate about the whole subject. Sometimes people aren't nice, you know!"

"Really? How terrible! What do they do?"

"Well, a man on the train today got up and moved after he found out what my button stands for. And a woman in Chichester spat at me." He grinned. "She missed."

"Really?" Barbara was amazed. "What awful manners!"

"Not everybody believes people should do what they want with their lives."

Of course, she thought to herself, *you do advertise what you are! And you have no right to corrupt children! They ought to put you away forever if you do that! And the world would come to an end if everybody was like you! They'd never get on with things—and then what would happen to the world?* "Lean here!" Barbara said to Jamie, whose nose was running. She took out some more paper towels from her purse and wiped away the mucus.

The young man had spotted the approaching dock. "We're almost there. *Wherever* it is we're going!" Barbara wondered what he meant by that odd remark. "It's been very pleasant talking with you," he said, lifting his overnight bag. "Can I help you with the baby carriage again?" He gestured at the pier.

"Oh, my husband will be meeting us."

"Well, goodbye then." The young man tapped his C.H.E. button. "It's nice to know there are some civilized people. It's a start."

"Yes, I do think people should try to be tolerant. Perhaps someday medical science will be able to help you," she said sincerely. "Come along, Neville! Daddy's here!" She waved to Mervyn waiting for them on the pier. "Neville, wave to Daddy! Come wave to Daddy!" She got the baby and held him up, waving his hand for him. Excitedly they all waved at one another.

Barbara looked at the solitary young man departing down the exit ramp by himself, and she was immensely thankful, so thankful, for everything she had, for what had been a quite happy, quite perfect day.

HIS VIEW

Jay was looking down at the suicidal waves dashing themselves against the pier, wondering if Martin would be waiting at Ryde when the ferry docked. It had been five days since they'd met in the gay bar and spent the night together. Now he'd be seeing Martin again, in his own setting, at work in the restaurant. It would be a marvelous two days before he left for Paris—wining, dining, and— His anticipation was interrupted by the sound of a mother yelling at a small boy who was about to push a baby carriage into the water. Jay ran over and grabbed the baby carriage and the child's hand. "Easy does it!" he said to the little boy, who looked up at him with fright.

In a moment the mother had reached them, retrieving her son, saying, "How can I ever thank you!"

"Don't worry about it," Jay replied. He noticed that the woman was almost out of breath with worry at the near accident. She was a chronic worrier, he could tell, big-boned and big-pelvised and as healthy as protein, but afraid of things, of the dangers lurking everywhere. She was looking from him to her son with a skittish smile on her face. Then she began scolding the boy in the sailor suit and scolding the infant in the baby carriage for tearing a shopping bag. She glanced up at the C.H.E. button he was wearing on a dare from Martin, who'd told him that despite the legality of homosexuality in England most people didn't talk openly about the subject—except with embarrassment.

"I only wear it to meetings myself!" Martin had explained.

"Well, I'll wear your button! It'll be *our* button!" Jay had joked as he was leaving Martin's hotel room.

"You wouldn't be so bold!" Martin had challenged.

"I'll wear it when I meet you at the dock in Ryde," Jay had promised. And here he was now—button, dare, and all!

"Are you an American?" the mother was asking him.

"Canadian!" *You'd think nobody but Americans existed!* Jay muttered to himself.

"Look, Mummy!" the small boy called out when the ferry's gangplank started to descend.

It looks like a gigantic tongue, Jay thought, *a gigantic tongue being stuck out to swallow all the passengers waiting to board.* It was a fanciful notion, and he knew he was enter-taining the idea merely to be "philosophical." *But before the big tongue licks me into oblivion I plan to get into Martin's bed one more time at least!* He spied several sea-gulls floating in the water at the rear of the docked ferry. They were waiting for bits of food to be thrown overboard.

"I've never been to the Isle of Wight before," Jay said to the young mother. "In fact, this is my first trip to Europe." He looked down at the seagulls in the bladelike waves again. *What must it feel like to be a seagull? Where do they fit into the scheme of things? Just floating in the waves, eating, day in and day out, until they die?*

Jay breathed in the sea air. *Being alive—that's the purpose of life, the only purpose, maybe.*

"Dirty! Dirty! Isn't he something!" the young mother was saying.

Preventing the eating of dog turds—is that the purpose of living?

"I couldn't help but notice your button," the young mother was saying, pointing to it.

"For Homosexual Equality." He felt self-conscious, but smiled. Another man stepping onto the gangplank turned his dignified head and gave Jay a distrustful stare. *I wonder what stereotypes that word conjures up?*

"Do you mind if I ask you why you wear a button about it?" She was valiant in her smile.

"So the subject will come up. I think it's about time the taboo died." Jay wasn't sure how his remark sounded. Argumentative? Pompous? He wasn't a militant and he hadn't decided what he'd say if the subject did come up, but if she wanted to talk about it, fine. If not, that was all right too. At least the next "homosexual" this woman met would be less frightening to her. *It's just that I'm tired of having to lie about where I'm going, who I'm seeing, what I'm thinking. She doesn't have to calculate each word carefully so she won't give herself away. She knows she's "right." She's the breeder. All I'd like is a little of her "rightness" for myself.*

He wanted to say more, but he didn't want to seem sharp with the woman. *I'm wearing a button—but just for today. Partly to see if I can do it, I guess. I'm not a "homosexual" all the time, only some of the time.*

"Would you like a sweet?" the woman was asking. It meant she wanted to talk, that she wasn't going to snub him. *We can talk of other things too. No need to embarrass her.*

But the older child began hiccuping and they couldn't talk. Jay saw an old couple looking in his direction and wondered if they took him for the father of the family. The idea pleased him, knowing it wasn't true. Or had the old couple heard them talking about his button and had their eyes on him as a kind of freak?

"They keep you busy, don't they?" he said, gesturing at the woman's children.

"Never a moment's rest!" She was busy patting the jam smears from around the baby's mouth, arguing with the older child about whether he could have a jam roll too.

Jay thanked the woman for the roll she'd given him, although it was sticky and slightly sour from the heat inside her large purse. Nor was the jam made of real strawberries, he noticed. Still he finished what he hadn't thrown to the seagull and licked his fingers clean. The feeling of salt and stickiness on his skin was exotic, vaguely uncomfortable and pleasant at the same time. *It would be wrong to wipe off the sensation. It'll be my special memory of this trip*, he thought. *My hands are more sensitive than my cock!* he teased himself. *That's why I love to sit at the potter's wheel, just holding my fingers cupped around the revolving clay, feeling the shapes fill in and hollow out, big-bellied and beautiful. To sit and feel the shapes emerge, to make as many beautiful ones as I can—beautiful, yes, but I don't really care about what they look like as much as how they feel on my hands when I'm making them!*

Jay sensed that the young mother was examining his back, and he turned around and caught her staring at his rear end with something like fear or distaste or dismay in her eyes. He hoped that she wasn't having a wave of revulsion about him. "Did you get to the Chichester Festival yet?" he enquired politely.

"Afraid we don't go."

Jay was surprised. The Festival Theatre was only a few miles away and she didn't go. He wondered if she and her husband went to the theatre in London, but he didn't ask, thinking he might embarrass her. Most likely they didn't. The woman seemed uncomfortable talking about not going, and he dropped the subject and mentioned his new contract with the gallery in Toronto.

"How interesting!" she said. "No, you don't, you little demon! You stay right here! You'll fall down the steps or something!" she said to the hiccuping child beside her, giving him a love-slap on his jaw.

"Say," Jay said, changing the subject, finding the conversation awkward since she seemed always distracted by her children, "maybe you can tell me what I should do while I'm on the Isle of Wight." He looked eagerly at the young mother, not intending in the least to follow her suggestions. Martin would know places to visit, but asking would make her feel she was an expert on something, even if she didn't go to the theatre or travel very far.

"They have some nice Mystery Tours. You go out on a fine, big bus without knowing where they're taking you. And they bring you back by four thirty. In time for tea!"

Jay was saddened. A mystery tour to nowhere. A mystery tour to someplace they'd been a dozen times before. And back for tea! Not even one night away! Back to get baby's formula ready. Back to tuck little Neville and little Jamie into bed. Back to sleep in Mervyn's familiar arms again. How sad it all was. How shiveringly sad and banal. "Maybe I'll take one of those then. Are they fun?"

"Oh, I'll have to change you as soon as we land," the mother was saying to the sleepy-looking child in the baby carriage. "My little tinkler! You!"

She felt to see if the baby's diaper was completely soaked, tickling his feet in passing. Jay felt melancholy again. How many times had this woman changed this baby's diaper? How many more would she change before he gained control of his bladder, of his bowels? How many had she changed for the other child? How many for the children yet to come? And what if the children merely grew up to reproduce themselves? What was all the effort, all her slavery for? Was that the "purpose"? Her hands must be wrinkled already, he suspected, although he couldn't see them, wrinkled and detergent-ruined and often pee-stained. Her hands full of soggy diapers and baby shit and jam rolls and half-chewed pieces of food, full of Tesco peas, and as for sex—her husband's monotonous penis on Wednesday and Saturday nights. How sad most of life was! How irretrievably bleak and regular, like logs in a saw mill.

"Have you ever tried to get a cure?" she abruptly asked him.

"A cure?"

"For what you mentioned before."

Do I look as if I need a "cure"? Is that what my dieting and exercising and bothering with being healthy get me!
"But you can't get a cure for what isn't an illness!" he said crisply. Spiteful words yearned to leap out at the woman: *Have you ever tried to get a cure for yourself! They make antibanality pills now!* Immediately he cooled down, but a gust of dislike passed over his mind. YOU'RE OBSESSED WITH HETEROSEXUALITY! ABSOLUTELY OBSESSED WITH IT!

"Oh, I'm sorry. I didn't mean to be insulting," the woman said, looking contrite. "But don't you get very lonely?"

He felt upset with himself for having been indignant. "There are lots of men like me. I meet them all the time." *I can't expect her to change in five minutes merely because she met me. How vain of me!* He was also annoyed with himself because he realized he was boasting about his sexual adventures. He knew he shouldn't boast, and yet how awful for this woman to have sex with the same person year in and year out, the predictable embraces, the numbing, humdrum rigidity of it all! How awful! How awful and how pathetic!

"Everybody should do what they want to do," the young woman was saying, still apologetic.

Jay was grateful for the centuries of civilization represented in her continued conversation with him. *After all, I've dealt her a pretty hefty challenge today. There is some progress,* he told himself hopefully. *There is! A few hundred years ago this same woman would've turned me over to the Inquisition. She would have screamed filthy names at me. I must be grateful that she's sitting here saying she's sorry.*

He watched her reach for another paper towel in her purse and wipe the snot from the infant's nose. *Snot and dog turds! We need your kind, attentive little mother, but not everybody has to be like you. Not every single one of us!* he said in silence. Aloud he said, "We're almost there. *Wherever it is we're going." Whatever the point of either of our destinations. The purpose of living is to live, I guess.* He smiled at her, his discomfort dissipating. "It's been very pleasant talking with you. Can I help you with the baby carriage again?"

"Oh, my husband will be meeting us."

"Well, goodbye then." Jay tapped Martin's C.H.E. button.

"It's nice to know there are some civilized people. It's a start." He raised his shoulders in an attempt at nonchalance.

"Yes, I do think people should try to be tolerant. Perhaps someday medical science will be able to help you."

Jay recoiled from the woman as if she'd given him a death sentence. *What a minimal start! We're grateful for crumbs, merely because they're not savage toward us!* he realized. She hadn't summoned the Inquisition or the Vice Squad or even walked away from him, but the depth of her condescension appalled and disgusted him. *She's sure that only her world matters. There isn't the slightest doubt in her mind that I'm absolutely inferior to her!*

Jay turned on his heel and strode away as the woman began telling her children to wave to their father on the pier. He looked back once at the waving hands, the mother's glowing, ripe cheeks. Suddenly in the midst of his hurt and fear, he felt extremely happy, the happiest he'd ever been in his life.

I'm free—as much as any human being can be free. I'm free and you're condemned to bear the burden of continuing the species. I'm free and you're not! And Jay's happiness tingled inside him.

a christmas miracle at the b.o.o.m.

"What do you suppose makes a guy gay?" Chet asked, wistful, swirling a swizzle stick around in his gin-and-tonic. He raised his dignified eyes, troubled. Then a smile twitched in one cheek, the cheek with the small Band-Aid where he'd nicked himself shaving.

"Who wants to find out? Let's just enjoy it," Graham said. He snuffed out his cigarette, taking his own medical advice. He pushed the ashtray away from them as the smoke curled up. "Are you sorry?" he asked Chet, wanting to touch his wrist to comfort him.

"No, I'm not sorry." Chet spoke in his best pilot's voice: decisive, firm, yet behind the authority was something mildly elegiac. "It's the best thing that's ever happened to me."

"You're nice."

"It's the truth."

"Have you told your wife yet?"

"She'll have to get used to it."

Graham didn't quite nod and looked across the dance floor at three dozen couples gyrating to the music that the Melting Pot was playing. The bandstand of the Officers Club was decorated with silver angels and red velveteen reindeer. Red-and-white streamers drooped from the ceiling.

"If your wife were here, maybe we could all dance to-gether—taking turns, of course," Graham snorted, nodding at the male-female couples having a good time on the dance floor. He noticed that he and Chet were the only people not dancing. But, after a moment, a laughing couple staggered off the dance floor, giggling into their booth a few tables away. The man, a captain that Graham worked with at Fifth Field Hospital, grabbed a streamer and broke it, then leaned down and kissed his partner, a Thai, sloppily on her neck.

"Now that they've left the floor, there's room for us to dance," Chet said, smiling over his drink.

Graham melted a little inside. *Chet's too perfect,* he thought. *Despite the freckles—lean, tall, and reasonably together. I've fallen in love with a homosexual fantasy. A doctor and a pilot—it's enough to—*

"*What* do you suppose they would say if we danced together?" Chet asked. He touched his cleft, aftershave-spiced chin with his thumb. "Huh?" His eyes burned for a moment.

"You start and I'll join you later."

Chet grinned. "Why is it that people aren't even allowed to dance alone?"

"Nobody's stopping you."

"If I danced by myself, everybody would stare."

"Mere custom."

"Yeah, 'mere custom.' Bet if I asked you to dance, they'd do more than stare." He pointed at Major Sullins, a man over fifty, with an unredeemable, bedraggled face, and shoulders as wide as the yoke on a water buffalo they'd seen in the rice paddies. "Old Sullins over there would grab his pistol and shoot us dead."

"Getting philosophical since you've come out?" Graham asked, hurting because he was the one who had brought Chet out.

"I guess I am. When I was straight, I never thought about it."

"Of course if we complain, we're nags. Nobody—" Graham's voice was drowned out by a gust of music, a hyped-up "Jingle Bells." Then somebody dressed in a Santa Claus suit entered the bar, with a large sack full of styrofoam padding over one shoulder.

"Ho! Ho! Ho! everybody!" he called, patting his big, holiday paunch. "Merry Christmas, everybody!" He grabbed the Thai waitress who was walking by and hugged her, almost spilling the drinks on her tray. The whole room laughed giddily at the Santa Claus, who squeezed the waitress again, until she disengaged herself and scurried to another section of the bar.

Then Santa, with difficulty because of his artificial bulk, jumped up onto the bar itself, casting multiple reflections of drunken Santa Clauses in the mirrors behind him. "Now who wants to come up here and sit on Father Christmas' knee?" he called to the room full of boisterous people. "Who wants to come and tell me what she wants for Christmas?"

A couple of women half-stood at their tables, wobbly with too much alcohol and merriment, as if they would go sit on Santa's knee. "I'll tell you what Sugar Daddy wants for *his* Christmas!" the man dressed as Santa roared. The crowd roared with him.

"Should I go tell him I want *you* for Christmas?" Graham asked, touching Chet's sleeve.

Chet turned his face toward him, not smiling. "You know you've already got that." He wanted to press Graham's hand on his arm, but he didn't dare.

Graham, against his will, looked around to see if anyone had overheard. It was a reflex. He had been doing it for all of his thirty-four years, it seemed. An Air Force doctor had to be on guard at all times, especially if he wasn't married. "You're the nicest Christmas present I've ever received," he said. "Or is that too sentimental?" He felt a tinge of self-consciousness.

"I'm in love with you," Chet said matter-of-factly.

Graham tingled somewhere in the recesses of his chest. He took a swallow of his brandy. "It won't last. It never does, of course."

"Yes, it will."

"Until tomorrow anyway. That's long enough." He said nothing more, not wanting to tell Chet, who at twenty-eight was inexperienced, that their love most likely *would* not last, that they would both go on to many other lovers and episodes. "It won't last, but that doesn't make it wrong *now*," Graham said, knowing that he couldn't be heard above the music.

The inebriated Santa Claus had jumped off the bar and was marching out of the room, followed by several others who were prancing like his reindeer. The Melting Pot played "God Rest Ye Merry, Gentlemen." Then, after a minute, the band was playing dance music again, and the male-female couples embraced each other once more.

"I want to dance with you," Chet persisted, moving his chair closer to Graham's. He put his hand under the tablecloth and squeezed the other's leg.

"Remember Major Sullins!" Graham warned him.

"Major Sullins be damned! I want to hold and kiss you!"

"A man wants to dance with another man! Jesus in his manger! What's the world coming to!" Graham said with mock horror.

Chet shrugged, squeezing the hidden leg again. "Someday we will."

"I doubt it." Graham caught a distant glimpse of Major Sullins' handsome teeth, the arm he had around his date. "Old Scrooge there will never have a conversion."

"Sure he will. Just goes to show how decadent we've become. Next thing you know, men'll be touching each other in public."

"I'd like to kiss you right now, right here."

Graham shook his head. "It'll never come true. Never." He tapped the edge of his brandy glass. "Can you imagine the two of us sitting holding hands in the Bangkok Officers Open Mess? Can you?"

"Let's make a wish on that," Chet gestured at the huge red tinselled star on top of the Christmas tree at the side of the bandstand. "What do you say, Doctor?" He stroked Graham's thigh.

Graham noticed another lieutenant colonel—another doctor—looking over in their direction, and he moved his leg. "You're insubordinate, captain!"

"Come on. Let's make a wish." Chet stuck both of his hands toward the star on the tall Christmas tree, which was decorated with faintly phallic baubles and white lights and strings of popcorn, and sprayed with soap that looked like snow. "I wish—I wish that we could always feel exactly the way we do right now."

Graham looked at the still-smoking cigarette in the ashtray. "Dorian Gray made a wish like that, and see what happened to him!"

"Come on," Chet coaxed. "Or I'll grab your leg again! Make the wish."

"Okay, okay. I wish that we won't forget each other's names two months from now!"

Chet looked disappointed. "You're bitter, aren't you?"

"I've been at this longer than you have."

"Even on Christmas Eve?"

"What better time? That's when people have to beware of slipping on candy canes. They're everywhere."

Chet looked at Graham's dark mustache, at the shadow below the lower lip, feeling unsettled and at peace at the same time. "Well, at least I got you to make the wish. Sort of."

"Maybe it will come partly true. Half a wish is better than none."

Chet grew more thoughtful again. "You know, if you did dance with me, we might start a trend."

"Or a war."

"If somebody doesn't fight back, nothing will ever change."

"You trying to earn a Purple Heart? You'll get one, that's for sure."

Chet looked down at his own large hands. "It would take more guts to dance with you than to drop a bomb on somebody."

"The Pilgrims of the Confraternity of St. Anne have to be careful."

Chet wrinkled his face. "*Pilgrims of St. Anne!* We have to resort to that kind of roundabout bullshit."

"Are you calling me a coward?"

"I'm only saying it would be a *brave* act to dance, strange as it may seem."

Graham made himself grin. "Know what? If you call a Chinese a coward, it isn't much of an insult. Civilized people, no? But Westerners will die rather than be thought cowardly." Graham ran his fingers over the coldness of his glass. "They teach you Southerners strange codes of honor, don't they?"

"Southern Illinois isn't the South."

"Same difference. You say 'sodee,' did you know that?"

"Are you changing the subject?" Chet said quietly.

"Of course I'm not. We'll *dance* for our country! And no doubt the Daughters of Gay Liberation one day will erect a monument to us. To our corpses."

"They might. You never know."

"I know."

"The plaque will read: To the Conquerors, Who Were Not Afraid."

"Only Major Sullins will come along with his machine gun and blast out the lettering, putting 'Goddamn Queers' there instead."

"I don't intend to stand by and let people push my face in."

Graham twisted in his chair uncomfortably. "Why do I always fall for pilots, do you suppose? Does that make me a Sky Queen?"

Chet didn't answer at first, then: "I'm not a 'queen' of any kind." He picked at the edge of the Band-Aid on his chin.

"Oh, don't be so uptight about being a little feminine. You probably like doctors—so you're an Ether Queen."

Chet's voice hardened. "*Somebody* has to be a man!"

"I doubt that our dance act would be interpreted as *manly*."

"Well, they're *wrong*, that's all!"

"Must be the heat in here." Graham waved his hand around in the flushed air, which seemed to hold too much, sagging with smoke and movement and music. "You'll learn to keep your tail between your legs, just like the rest of us, stud."

Chet loosened his tie. "I wasn't a sissy before. Why should I be one now?"

"Nobody would ever think you're a sissy," Graham said, sensing Chet's growing anger. "Let's not spoil the Christmas spirit, okay?" He flicked one finger on Chet's wrist.

Chet glared across at the drunken officer and his Asian date, who had rejoined the throbbing dancers in front of the bandstand. "That little banty rooster and his concubine can get up there and throw their bodies at each other. But we have to sit here. It's—"

"We can't have everything." Graham manipulated a shin past the other's kneecap. "Besides, I've got enough. I've got you."

"We're supposed to be content with a sneaky pinch under the table?"

"Whoa, mister! Slow down!"

24

Chet took a long swallow of his drink. "What *would* they do?" He slammed the glass down. "If we got up for a slow dance, do you think the others would bump into us? Try to separate us? Would the club manager intervene?"

"All of those," Graham snickered. "And don't forget Officer Scrooge—he'd get grenades. And they'd court-martial the fragments."

"Merry Christmas to all. And to all a good night!" Chet said harshly, his glass lifted, toasting the room.

Across the way Major Sullins noticed the toast and yelled "Merry Christmas" back.

"What time is it?" Graham asked.

Chet looked at his watch. "A quarter to twelve."

"In fifteen minutes we'll have been in love a week."

"Is that a record?"

"At this velocity, yes." Graham didn't say the words easily; he'd always snorted when he'd heard people trading lovers' endearments. They made him suspicious, faintly nauseous. But now he understood the impulse to tell the loved one, to tell and tell and tell again.

"We could go up to my room and make love," Chet said.

"Sodomy on Christmas?" Graham teased.

Chet studied him, the upper lip that drooped ever so slightly, the black eyes that never seemed rested, even in the morning. "Why is it homosexuals are so often bitchy?"

"Am I bitchy?"

"There's a streak there."

"You're right. You have the unjaded eye of the neophyte." He bowed, chin to chest. "I suppose we're bitchy because that's where our frustrations go—if you're seeking my professional medical opinion."

"Don't you ever get fed up pretending to be straight, making up stories to deflect suspicion from yourself?"

Graham shook his head in agreement. "So sick you wouldn't believe."

"And I used to make antifag jokes all the time!" Chet pushed on both temples, to show his self-disgust.

"Just don't turn bitchy. Promise me."

"I don't intend to."

"Of course it makes us witty, but it's not our most becoming trait. Self-hate can begin to stink like . . . like former lovers."

"I suppose being bitchy isn't as bad as raping peasants, is it?"

Graham smiled. "Hey, *heavy* . . ."

Chet punched his forehead. "I'm beginning to get tired of thinking about it all." He gestured at those on the dance floor. "*They* don't have to analyze and analyze."

"They have to pay; they have to raise their children. I only have to swab their throats occasionally."

"It's unfair."

Graham leaned nearer. "No, you're supposed to say: 'I'd love to have you swab *my* throat sometime.' The perfect erotic lover. We're supposed to take our resentment out in sex, got it?"

"We've got as much right as anybody else!"

Graham took the swizzle stick out of Chet's drink and snapped it. "Tell the truth. Wouldn't you be shocked out of your mind if you saw two fags snuggling up in a public place? Be truthful."

"Sure I would. But I'd get used to it. Fast."

"It takes time—a time of liberality for the barriers to drop enough in order for a few changes in sexual mores to occur. What happens is that the homosexuals can then venture a daring kiss or two, a squeeze under the table, let's say— because of the greater 'liberality.' But at the same time other barriers are cracking—rapes and corruption, for instance. So we fags get blamed for the growing 'immorality'— you know, like in Rome. We're all lumped together, when all we are really is one of the offshoots of the general increase in freedom."

"What was that again?"

"Never mind—I must be drunk." Graham finished his brandy. "I was never that articulate, really, only superficially."

"I think you're fine just the way you are."

"That's what lovers always say—just before they begin to make 'slight revisions' in the beloved."

"Really? What are you going to change me into?"

"I'm going to make you shave closer before we hop into

bed." Graham held his face rigid, before letting the smile slide into view.

"Do I irritate you, so to speak. Even though I shave close?" He touched the Band-Aid.

Graham leaned over and grasped Chet's forearm with his whole hand. "Oh God! Why can't we stay like this forever?" He looked over at the Christmas tree star—a bright red. "Why must it turn into something else, something bitter, something crumbling at the edges, the way it did with Ron."

"It doesn't have to happen."

"Maybe. It's just that almost everything turns sour. The Christmas goodies we're whispering to each other will get stale, or become crumbs in the bottom of the box." Graham tried to smile, knowing he was taking himself too seriously. "It just will, that's all. On *that* we can depend. My patients will continue to break their bones and get diaper rash and lovers will continue to fall out of love. It's built into the system."

"I bet if we held each other on the dance floor, beneath the big Christmas tree, we'd never change." Chet didn't believe them, but he said the words anyway.

Graham felt a surge of passion, a longing mixed with melancholy. If only he and Chet really could stay the way they were!

The music changed to a slow number, or perhaps it had been slow for some time. Graham had not really been listening to the music. He glanced at the dance floor and saw that there were only half a dozen couples left. The others had left the bar or returned to their tables. Would he dare?

"Let's dance," Chet said, staring into Graham's eyes.

Suddenly Major Sullins was upon them, having stumbled from his table to theirs. He clapped Chet on the back. "Hey, Swigert, you having a good time?" His face was sun-doused, as clean as a new airplane engine part, hair like gray brush bristles.

"Can't complain," Chet said.

"No dates, you two—on Christmas Eve?"

"Afraid we've just got each other—Graham and I."

"That's not much!"

Chet did not hate Sullins; he was too banal to waste such

emotions on, simply one of the impediments that had to be put up with if one stayed in the military. Maybe it was time for him to get out. Six years was enough. He stared up at the desperate-to-have-a-good-time, uncomplicated face of Sullins, and wondered if he had a right to ask Graham to give up his eight and a half years in the Air Force too.

"Guess you two'll have to dance together," Sullins joked, exploding, but not grossly enough. Chet grinned; he wanted to hate the man. There should have been some spit on his lip. Or he should belch, to complete the hatred. But such satisfying patterns were rare in life.

"Yeah, guess we'll have to," Chet said, standing up. "You know how it is when you're in love. You do foolish things." He looked at the Thai woman that Sullins had left alone. Then he looked down at Graham. "You want to dance?" He held out his hand.

Major Sullins fell backwards with amusement. Recovering, he winked. "Now if he kisses you, don't giggle!"

"I won't giggle," Graham said, biting on the words. He looked up at Chet, whose hand was still extended. *I can always practice medicine somewhere else. And it's time to get out*, he thought. He rose and pushed back his chair. "Reporting for duty. Permanent, I hope." He nodded at Chet. "All right, mister, let's dance."

He and Chet walked to the dance floor. Both had begun to sweat, but Graham closed his eyes as they encircled their arms around each other. Chet closed his eyes too. Then, catching the rhythm of the slow music, they pressed together and began to dance. In the near distance they could hear Sullins uproarious with hilarity, but neither Chet nor Graham opened his eyes to look.

"Whoopee! Aren't we sweet!" Sullins' voice said. He still believed they were joking. Two of the men dancing with their dates muttered something too, and a woman cackled dizzily.

"Get a load of that!" Sullins shouted, pointing.

"How you doing?" Chet said as he whirled Graham around, his leg between his partner's legs.

"So far, so good." Graham felt a gob of sweat grab at his throat. When he opened his eyes, he saw that other couples on the floor were staring at them, as were people at the tables. The Thai waitresses were smiling, poking one another.

"What a couple of clowns!" Major Sullins called, jovially, going along with the joke.

"We're quite amusing," Graham said into Chet's ear.

"I don't feel funny at all," Chet answered. "I'm not going to back down now."

"You dance great," Graham said.

Major Sullins took a step onto the dance floor, waving at the band. "Give these fags some better music than that! I want to see 'em jitterbug!"

The music flared into a rock and roll number, but when Chet and Graham continued to dance slowly, ignoring it, the band returned to the original music. Out of the corner of his eye Graham noticed the couples looking at them were no longer smiling.

"Okay, ladies, that's enough now!" Major Sullins called to them. His grin had disappeared too. "You guys were a scream!"

Chet and Graham ignored him.

"Okay, knock it off!" a surly voice said from a booth in the shadows.

"You've had your laugh!" someone else yelled.

Graham started to unclasp Chet, but Chet held him and would not release him. He could feel the other's warm breath on his chin.

"We're not going to stop. Ever!"

"Okay, fellows, cut out the shit! What do you think you're doing!" an anonymous voice cut into them.

Graham took a deep breath. "I think I can hear Sullins putting cartridges into his pistol."

"No, that's just the ice in his glass."

Graham looked beyond Chet's head and noted the frowns on a few faces. The other dancers had moved farther away from them.

"HEY! Knock it off, I said!" Major Sullins yelled, taking a step closer, even though Graham outranked him. He was only a few yards away, and they continued to move around the dance floor, very aware of their blue uniforms.

"Let's make a wish on that big red star," Chet whispered into Graham's ear.

He nodded, and together they focussed on the top of the

Christmas tree and made the wish. They held each other fiercely, and when they looked again the other couples were no longer frowning.

"They're . . . they're not going to stop us," Graham said.

Even Major Sullins had gone off to another table to wish someone a Merry Christmas.

Graham hugged his lover. "God bless you, Captain Vere!" he said ironically.

Chet didn't catch the jest, but he laughed, "God rest ye merry, gentleman!" he grinned back.

And, dazed, afraid to let go of each other lest the moment be broken, they danced on and on. Time held its breath, and Christmas Eve never ended.

This is the only miracle ever known to have occurred in the Bangkok Officers Open Mess.

two bartenders, a butcher, and me

I'd just got over a bad case of meningitis, complicated by my diabetes, and my doctor had told me the day before that I was probably getting kidney stones too. (Nobody knows what pain is until he has kidney stones, believe me.) So when the guy from San Francisco stared at me in the bar and then came over and asked if I wanted to join in an orgy, you can understand why I felt good. I realized I must look a bit puny with my thin shoulders and thinner arms, my fat lips and dwindling hair (though I'd cut it flat to make it look less obvious). But the guy from San Francisco was making the overture, saying he and his lover, Gil, were arranging an orgy. They'd already asked the bartender if he wanted to have a four-way, and the bartender had said he did. I guess they liked my face. It turned out that Gil was a bartender too—up in San Francisco, not here in Fresno—and for a minute all four of us sort of eyed each other, seeing how we felt about getting together.

To be honest, the Fresno bartender, Rory, didn't turn me on very much. He was cute and growing a nice beard, but somehow he seemed a little silly. (I'd seen him running around the bar lots of times before, but we'd never spoken.) Gil was pretty good-looking, far better than me in fact, with elegant gestures and a deep voice. The best of the lot was the guy from San Francisco, a butcher, who was slim and solid and lots of fun. Up close, he looked a little dissipated, because of the dark marks under his eyes. That night he'd had about six White Russians and had been smoking grass and even sniffed some amyl out on the dance floor, so I wondered if I would be getting in over my head by getting into an orgy with those guys. But the guy from San Francisco, Bill, was really full of life and having a great time running back and forth between the three of us, finding out who liked to do what.

I began to get sleepy before the bar closed and thought of leaving, since I had to get up and go to work at the Welfare Department in the morning at eight. But somehow or other I hung in there. I was going to lose my job anyway in a couple of months, because the budget had been cut, but I didn't want to lose it for coming in worn-out from an all-night orgy. Still, I kept asking myself how many offers for an orgy at the Fresno Holiday Inn did I get in a year, anyway.

So I waited around while the two guys from San Francisco danced and the bartender closed up. I was getting a little worried because I don't have a very big dick and Bill talked about cock a lot, as though size was very important to him. I didn't want him to be disappointed when I pulled my pants off. (I know it's not supposed to matter if you have a little dick, but it does, it sure does.) I tried looking over at Rory, but he didn't catch my eye, and I figured he wasn't attracted to me any more than I was to him. But I also figured a three-and-a-half-way was better than a no-way, so I hung in there.

Somehow some Italian guy got involved. He was supposed to make up a fifth in the orgy, but when we left the bar I found out, in the parking lot, that Rory had lost interest in the Italian and didn't want him to follow us in our cars out to the Holiday Inn. I felt sorry for the Italian because he didn't catch the hint and followed us all anyway, and then, at the motel, Rory had to lie and say that all of us were action "so weird" that he didn't plan to stay. So the Italian guy was left out in the cold. I guess he went on home.

The other four of us went into the motel room and took our clothes off. There was a big tray of dirty dishes and half-eaten food on one of the double beds, and the beds were unmade and clothes were thrown everywhere. It was all a little messy, but I suppose you wouldn't want an orgy to be middle-class and super-clean anyway, right?

I didn't know exactly what I was supposed to do, but the butcher gave me a sniff of amyl and asked me to fuck him while Rory was fucking him too. It was pretty wild, I guess. It was the first time I'd ever seen a guy get fucked with two cocks at the same time—and I was one of the guys doing it! I kept thinking about the Italian who'd been invited and then not invited, wondering if he was still in the parking lot, sitting in his car by himself. Of course, I hadn't said anything to the others about asking the Italian to join us, so I guess I made him feel not wanted, too.

So we all fucked each other in various combinations, though Rory and I didn't touch very much, just a little bit near the end. And nobody said anything about my little dick, though I think Bill was maybe a little disappointed. But if I have to defend myself, he couldn't have been fucked by me and somebody else at the same time if we'd both had big ones.

When I got off, I was sitting on Gil's dick, and the other two were watching from the other bed, even encouraging me to come. I suppose if anybody had been watching from a peephole it would've seemed nasty or depraved or something, but it didn't seem like that from my angle. We even joked around a lot and hugged and told each other we were good sex. We got so loud that Bill shushed us and said we'd wake up his mother. I thought he was kidding, but it turned out he wasn't. His mother really *was* in the next room. She was travelling with them, and she knew about him and Gil and took it all with a grain of salt, though she wouldn't talk about it.

The moment I remember most is when Rory, who was really quite a good fucker, was giving it to Bill, who had his legs up in the air and was grunting. Gil and I were resting on the rug and Gil says to me, quietly, "I really love him. I love him so much." He meant it, too, and I thought that was sort of nice. Here he was watching some bartender from Fresno fucking his lover in the ass and he was glad because it gave his lover pleasure.

About four-thirty I slipped out and left the other three sleeping. Didn't get a chance to say goodbye. I got to work on time (still have a month to go in my job and I can get unemployment for a while after that).

For some reason that evening didn't seem funny or depraved or anything. All I know is that when I was sucking dick and getting fucked and fucking that night, I didn't feel like I was a skinny thirty-eight-year-old with a little dick that nobody wanted. Of course I knew that nobody there in the Holiday Inn "loved" me, but for a while I felt that life wasn't passing me by, and I guess I'm kind of wishing some guy from San Francisco would come on through Fresno some other night, maybe soon. It wasn't perfect, no, but it was *something*. Maybe it was even sort of sad if you think about it too much, but then, aren't most things in life sad?

his little rabbit

"Oh, my God, I'm so happy!"

"So am I," Jean-Claude said.

"If someone had told me a year ago I'd be living with a Frenchman I'd have laughed in his face—or shrugged my shoulders," I said, tickling Jean-Claude. "But you're not typical. Of course."

He touched my face and then reached down for the tube of lubricant near my thigh. I watched the supple, brown flesh on his ribcage tighten as he leaned toward the night-stand, and I felt a thrill of desire again. I put my hand on his soft back and ran it across the two dimples in his shoulder blades, then across his neck. The body was solid and tanned, the skin like an expensive, cool fabric. The stomach puffed out, but it didn't matter. I was in love with a human being, not a photograph of a demigod. I picked up his hand and placed it hard on my chest.

"What's the matter, Will?" he asked.

"I just want you to touch me."

"My last lover also liked the massage on his chest."

" 'Last lover'—what an awful term," I said. "I don't want to hear about him."

"Oh, you Americans are such romantics, and it's the French who have the reputation."

"Sometimes I think you're not French at all. Only pretending."

Jean-Claude slowly stroked the bridge of my nose. "Why do you say this?"

"You're the only Frenchman I've met who didn't speak like ziz and speak like zat!"

35

"We speak your impossible language, and then you make fun of us for doing it!"

"I know—we're terrible. How do you put up with us?"

"Oh, you have your good qualities." He gave my butt a spank.

I turned, in order to hold his slippery cock in both hands, then shook it. "It isn't just sex, I hope!"

Jean-Claude waved the back of his hand at me and shook his head. "You always get coy when we have this . . . chitchat after sex. It's almost part of the orgasm." He patted my butt. "But I suppose that is all right. That is the way it is."

I looked at his face. I hadn't been attracted to him at first—the receding, usually damp hairline, the irregular jaw, the intense black-green eyes, like some night animal's. He must have been close to fifty too, although well-preserved. But I'd gradually fallen in love with his personality—like a dog hypnotized by a trainer who's sometimes tender, sometimes cruel.

Suddenly I looked at my own body—the legs hard from hiking, the arms muscular, with the vein prominent in each one, the bellybutton like a corkscrew. Jean-Claude had told me many times that he found me attractive . . . but I didn't want him to want me for the way I looked. "Do you . . . love me?" I said.

"I've asked you to live with me, haven't I?" He pointed at his bedroom with the expensive woodcuts on the wall. "And I share my big bed with you." He clutched a handful of blankets near my head and grinned. "And you wear my slippers." He pointed at the green slippers I'd dropped beside the bed.

"You're avoiding the question," I said.

"Oh! I know *you*, Monsieur! You're the kind that takes for granted whatever comes too easy!"

I sat up against the headboard. "You think that's true!"

"Of course." He lifted my hand and kissed the palm. "You have many wrinkles in here."

"Can you read palms?" I asked him, looking at my lifeline.

"Anyone can tell fortunes . . . only they are not reliable." He took my hand and examined it.

"What do you see . . . about us?"

"Here's your love line," he said, tracing his finger across the skin. "It's very tangled."

"That's not so."

Jean-Claude smirked. "What do you want me to tell you?"

"The truth."

"Don't be foolish. Nobody wants the truth."

He looked at me with deadly sincerity, and I shivered.

"Cold?" He drew the covers up around me, although he stayed outside them himself.

"I care a lot about you," I said, unable to look directly at him.

"Ah, my little cabbage," he said, chucking me under the chin like a cartoon Frenchman.

"Well, you *like* me at least?"

"Oh, you make everything so important! Life is not that way! Take it more like it comes."

"You're the first man I've ever . . . cared for."

He chuckled. "Ah, *mon p'tit lapin*, you can be so very nice."

"What does *mon p'tit lapin* mean?"

"My little rabbit."

I grinned. "I'm thirty-three and no one ever called me his little rabbit before." I shivered again.

Jean-Claude lay on top of me, with the covers between us. "Are you catching pneumonia? Are you going to make me sick?"

"I don't know why I'm shivering."

"It's love," he said, breathing right into my eyes. He smelled good. "Love makes us hot. And love makes us cold."

I felt uneasy being teased and yet liked it too. I turned and looked at the shifting images of the TV screen. We had turned the sound off.

"Do you think this is one of the happiest moments of our lives?" I asked.

"Because?"

"Being in love. Both of us in love, I mean." I put my hands over his face and felt the soft hollows beneath his eyes, the prickly stubble along his jaw. "You *do* love me too, right?" I said.

"Oh, my little *lapin*, you want everything spelled out," Jean-Claude answered, and then kissed me between the eyes.

We got out of the car with the picnic basket between us. "All right?" Jean-Claude asked, gesturing at the marina.It was almost deserted, except for an old woman walking her old dachshund, its belly dragging on the ground. On the water itself there was a solitary water skier in the distance.

We sat among some willow trees on a small mound, and Jean-Claude removed the cork from the wine bottle—without so much as a spilled drop—and handed me a plastic glass full of white wine.

"It's beautiful here," I said, meaning the trees and grass.

"You're looking very splendid yourself," he said, toasting me with his glass.

"Our anniversary?" I asked. "Six months." I swallowed the wine too fast, and it chilled the back of my throat.

"Has it been six months?" he said, taking some cheese out of the picnic basket—some Camembert—and spreading it on the crackers. He handed me one.

"Who's counting!" I said with a false laugh. I realized that he'd brought me there to talk seriously. We hadn't had sex for three weeks. And the last time had obviously been unpleasant for him. "Well, here we are!" I said, sipping the wine again. A hundred yards away the old woman was sitting at a picnic table feeding dog biscuits to the fat dachshund.

I opened the picnic basket and lifted out the tuna salad sandwiches I'd made. "Want one?"

"Only some cheese," Jean-Claude answered. "But you go ahead."

I unwrapped the cellophane and bit into the sandwich. Some of the filling squished out, but I caught it before it fell. Jean-Claude and I both laughed, as though we were having a good time. "It's sort of like our second honeymoon, isn't it?" I said.

"We never had a first, so this cannot be the second," Jean-Claude said.

I took another bite and refilled my glass. "You have a way

of beating around the bush," I smiled.

Jean-Claude sat cross-legged on the grass and popped a piece of cracker into his mouth. It was a very handsome mouth—his best feature by far. A friendly mouth with a horizontal line cut in the lower lip. He'd grown a mustache and the silvery hairs almost covered it. The black-green eyes were wonderful, looking at me intently, waiting for the proper moment to tell me why he'd arranged this picnic.

But I looked away from the eyes, and stretched out on my side. If I didn't let him say the words, then the affair would go on. It could go on for another year at least, I was sure.

"Are you comfortable, Will?"

"What the executioner said before he dropped the blade of the guillotine, yes?" I said.

"You are very . . . aggressive, in words," Jean-Claude said slyly.

"We journalists can outflank you scientists any day," I said.

"No doubt," he said, touching his lips with one finger. A bit of sunshine fell across his knees.

"See that old woman all alone?" I asked. "Sort of sad, isn't she?"

"Perhaps you make her seem more sad than she is—in your mind, I mean."

I looked at his eyes, like dark jewels. "Perhaps I do. maybe she's really very happy. Almost as happy as me, living with someone. With *you*, I mean."

"Are you really happy living with me?" Jean-Claude said, looking at me like a judge.

"You don't see me trying to get out of it . . ."

He knelt and poured some more wine into my glass. "*Why* are you happy?"

The question caught me by surprise. "Well, because— because we go to movies together. The theatre. Ah . . . we talk at breakfast . . . Sex."

"Yes, we have had good sex sometimes . . ."

I put my plastic glass between my legs, near my crotch, so that he would look at it. "Thank you. I needed that."

"Perhaps you have noticed I have been restless some days."

I paused deliberately. "I have . . ."

"I'm not sure that . . . domestic—that I'm at my best—how do you say?—'settled down' . . ."

"I've never held a gun to your head about being faithful . . ."

"Never." He looked in the picnic basket for something else, but took nothing out.

"I packed some carrot cake," I said. "Want some?"

Jean-Claude waved his hand over the basket. "I don't like sweets. You know that."

"That's right. I know that." Something icy rippled up my back. It was probably the wind from the marina, I told myself.

He sat back down and stared at me, until I felt the tuna salad stick in my mouth. "This picnic is going to help us get back together again, isn't it, Jean-Claude?" I said, putting my hand near my fly.

He looked at me with tenderness in his deadly green-black eyes. "You're very sexy," he said. "You should have no trouble finding somebody else."

I was sitting alone in the movie theater during the interval when someone tapped my shoulder.

"So how are you getting along, Will?"

I turned and saw Jean-Claude sitting behind me. His mustache had grown into a silvery beard trimmed close to his face. He was wearing his glasses with the thin metal rims. "Were you sitting there all the time?"

"We just came in." He indicated the other man. "This is my friend Dennis."

"Hi," I said, barely registering Dennis, who seemed attractive, lean, in his midtwenties. I looked back at Jean-Claude, who was wearing a blue wool shirt with the sleeves rolled up. It was the first time I'd talked to him since I'd moved out of his apartment. Something went hot and numb in my head, and I felt such a burst of longing I almost blacked out.

"You never call," Jean-Claude said. "We cannot still be friends?"

"Oh, I've been very busy," I lied. "How have you been?" I was aware of the grin sticking to my face. The smell of marijuana drifted over from the smoking section.

"I am fine—I got a promotion. I am a senior chemist now."

"Oh, that's great!" I wondered if Dennis could tell I could barely see either of them because I was so blurry-headed. I went on smiling furiously. The other movie patrons would think nothing was wrong, just three friends talking.

"And how about *your* career?" Jean-Claude said. "I saw that article you did on fuels. Very good."

"I almost called you about that—to verify some facts, that is. But I thought you'd be busy."

He leaned over and whispered into my ear. "I hope you are not angry with me."

"Of course not—you treated me very well."

He put his strong hand on my neck and squeezed. "Did you find a place to live? You should have let me help—"

"Oh, it was easy—I have a nice little studio."

"That is what you want?"

"It's really nice."

"You should invite me over." He sat back in his seat. "And Dennis too."

I looked at Dennis again. He resembled me in a way, but with a better proportioned body. Big warm eyes and slim hips. There was a luster in his eyes that showed he was intelligent. Suddenly I hated Dennis. I could see him and Jean-Claude wrapped in each other's arms, their tongues touching . . .

"Are you going to stay for both movies?" Dennis asked.

"No, just the one with Alan Bates."

"Yes, he's terrific," Dennis said.

"Are you two . . . living together?" I asked, afraid of the answer.

Jean-Claude laughed. "Oh, no, we just met. When was it?" He looked at Dennis.

"Two or three weeks ago," Dennis said.

I felt a rush of relief, and I looked at Jean-Claude again. I wanted him to touch me. I hadn't had anything except some stand-up sex in a backroom since we'd stopped being lovers. I wanted to lie in his bed with his body on top of mine, to have him touch me, to caress me, his strong, warm hands all over me. My whole body felt brittle, as if it would shatter if

41

Jean-Claude didn't warm it right that moment.

I felt my eye twitch—a tic, and I put my hand over it.

"Something wrong?" Jean-Claude asked.

"A speck of dirt."

He stood up and came around to the seat next to mine, annoying a couple who had come down the aisle to sit in the empty seats near me.

"Let me see," he said.

"It's all right."

He pried my fingers away from my face and studied my eye. I could feel it jump, as if something had broken loose.

"I do not see anything," he said gently.

"It's gone."

He held onto my forearms, sitting just a few inches away from my eye, and my body filled with a cruel, cold heat. I exerted all my will to keep my eye from jumping.

"I've been under a lot of pressure on my job," I lied.

"Oh, you take everything too seriously. I always said that!" He patted my forehead, then went back to his seat. The house lights were starting to go down, and someone took the seat beside me, an old man with a pungent odor.

As soon as the movie started, I heard Jean-Claude laugh—a rich laugh, but somewhat mocking too.

How can you *make* somebody love you? I said to myself.

"You must come and visit. Or we must have lunch one day," Jean-Claude said later, when I got up to leave.

How can you make somebody love you? I wondered.

"I'm going to be in your neighborhood, and I thought I might stop by. If you're free," I said.

"Right now?" Jean-Claude's voice on the telephone sounded sleepy.

"But if you're not free . . ."

"Excuse me. I was just taking a nap, that is all. I would love to see you, Will."

"Only if you promise to treat me like a special guest," I joked.

"I will make tea for you, how's that? And my mother sent me some biscuits from France."

"What are you wearing right now?" I said.

"*Pardon?*"

"Let's pretend this is an obscene phone call. You tell me that you're standing there in the nude and I . . ." All of a sudden I became embarrassed by my own joke.

"I am lying here in the nude, as a matter of fact."

"Are you playing with yourself?"

"*Garce!*"

"Well, *are* you?" I pictured his handsome cock, the almost rosy flush to it when it was excited, the foreskin pulled back.

"I will make tea for you, all right?" Jean-Claude said, and hung up.

I still had a key and let myself into the apartment. "Anybody here?" I called up the long staircase with the thick carpeting.

"Only me," a voice said. I looked up and saw Dennis holding onto the white railing. His chest was bare; he had a slim body with dark hairs in a swirl around the nipples. I couldn't see his legs because there was a bath towel drying on the railing.

"Is Jean-Claude home?" I asked.

"He had to go out for some tea. Turns out he didn't have any." Dennis came down a few steps to greet me, wearing Levi's. "Welcome!" He put his arms around me and gave me a friendly kiss on the cheek. I could smell mint deodorant or aftershave on his skin. "You'll have to excuse me. I haven't finished dressing yet." He led me down the hallway. "Make yourself comfortable. Living room's in there." He pointed.

Softly I said, "Yes, I remember."

"That's right, you used to live here!" Dennis said, folding his arms. His flesh was tight and flawless like a melon's, I noticed. He started to leave the room but stopped. "I was making the bed, but I suppose it can wait." He came back and sat on the arm of the sofa, opposite me. Had he and Jean-Claude been making love when I called? . . . Had they continued after Jean-Claude had hung up?

"So you're living here now, Dennis?" I asked, overinterested.

"Just for a month or two, most likely. Till I get settled in my new job. Jean-Claude suggested it."

I put my arm nonchalantly on the back of the chair I was

sitting in. "Oh, what's the new job?"

"A dishwasher at the moment. That's what a B.A. in Latin will get you in this town." He grinned, almost boyishly, but there was some resentment in his words too.

"Were you in the seminary?"

"Jesuit."

"Well, I'm sure you'll work up to something better than dishwashing."

"My boss has already said I can be a waiter in a couple of weeks. Somebody's leaving."

Dennis was charming, I could see that now. A little bitter, but lively and basically good-natured. He didn't quite look me in the eye—out of shyness, I felt.

"Can I get you something until the tea arrives?"

"I'm fine," I said. I looked down and noticed that he was wearing Jean-Claude's old green slippers. The ones I had worn when I'd lived there.

"Gee, we haven't seen you since that time at the movie, have we? When was that?"

"About six weeks ago."

"Jean-Claude and I weren't even lovers then, were we?"

"That's what you said at the time," I managed.

Dennis must have caught something in my voice, because he looked embarrassed. "I've read some of your newspaper articles, and I've been very impressed," he said.

"Thank you."

There was a clumsy pause.

I felt almost drunk—drunk and dehydrated at the same time. "Do you and Jean-Claude sleep together in the big bed?" I asked, unable to stop myself.

Dennis hesitated. "Yes . . . usually."

"Jean-Claude's great to sleep with, isn't he? Hardly moves all night."

"That's right."

"He was the only person I was ever able to sleep with, isn't that strange?"

"Yes, he's an—"

The downstairs door opened, and Jean-Claude's voice called up. "Hello! I'm back! Hello!"

"Hello!" I called.

"I have the tea, *lapin*," Jean-Claude said, rushing up the stairs.

So I was still *lapin*, I thought, aching to see him. I got up. Then he saw me. "Oh, excuse me! I thought that was Dennis's voice," he said, shaking my hand, then kissing Dennis between the eyes.

I called Jean-Claude at work the next day. "Well, how's the senior chemist doing?" I said.

"He's very busy. And how are you?"

". . . I won't keep you long. Just wondered how you are—and wanted to thank you for the tea party last night."

"I enjoyed myself too."

"Dennis seems very nice."

"He seemed to like you also."

"I'm sorry if I seemed a little . . . distracted or anything."

Jean-Claude waited, then said, "Perhaps a little bit."

"Must be that old Gallic charm of yours." Could he tell I wanted him? Would I make a fool of myself if I said any more?

"Are you seeing anybody, Will?"

"Oh, I've given up all that," I said, trying for lightness. "Celibacy is the latest thing, haven't you heard?"

"What you need is . . . but who am I to give advice!"

Why do I want you even though you don't want me? I said to myself. I want to be free of you! I want to be free!

"My job is getting to be too much," Jean-Claude said. "They have given me now two new projects and I'm not finished with the last one yet!"

"What are they?"

"Oh, it's too technical to go into," he said, but he went on explaining. I felt the telephone receiver against my ear, and I remembered that Jean-Claude could be heavy, even tedious, going into details about chemistry that meant nothing to me. And yet I found even his tediousness erotic—something solid and stable. His voice was full of chemical compounds and memories of the way he used to whisper for me to get undressed.

". . . to cure eczema," Jean-Claude was saying.

"I suppose with your new projects and Dennis and everything you're pretty busy," I broke in.

"Did you like Dennis? He's very special, don't you think?"

"Oh . . . very nice, yes."

"And—excuse me for saying this—he's very sexy. Keeps me active, *toujours*!" Jean-Claude snickered and I felt something frigid slither in my belly. "He seems to think that sex was just invented. I have—"

Shut up! Shut up! You've fallen in love with Dennis! "He's your little cabbage, it sounds like," I laughed.

"I am afraid I'm getting too fond of him."

I could see a dim reflection of myself in the window near the telephone: Dark-peach beard and darker eyebrows, a good nose, a pleasant ass. Jean-Claude, why don't you love me anymore? Dummy! I told myself. As if it's flesh alone! Do I even want your "love"? Do I just want you back because *you* rejected me? If this is "love," why does anybody want it? It's too painful, too painful . . .

"Well, I'd better be going now," Jean-Claude said. "Are you at work?"

"I'm at home. I'm supposed to be doing a story on grasshoppers, of all things." Don't hang up yet, please!

"Well, we must see each other. Of course."

"Maybe without Dennis sometime . . ." Does Jean-Claude know my mind? If I ask and he refuses . . .?

"Ah, well, Dennis and I are together most of the time now."

"Be careful! You know what happens when you over-indulge in anything."

"I'll be careful . . ."

I coughed. "Did we have too much sex, Jean-Claude? Is that what went wrong?"

". . . There is no time to talk about this now, Will."

"But I must have done something! All of a sudden you didn't want to make love to me anymore. Almost overnight."

"Do you really want to know?"

My heart froze. No, I didn't really want to know. "Perhaps some other time," I said.

"You were very nice in many ways, Will . . . many ways."

"Who knows, maybe we'll click again sometime," I ventured, holding my breath.

"Well, I really must get back to work now," Jean-Claude said.

"Hello? Jean-Claude?"

"No, this is Dennis."

"Oh hello, Dennis. I didn't recognize your voice."

"Is this Will?"

"You recognize my vibrations?" I said.

"You have a very distinctive voice," he said.

"Thank you. I take it Jean-Claude's out?"

"He went to a meeting. About chemistry or something."

"That's Jean-Claude, isn't it?"

"What's new with you, Will?"

"Oh, I'm taking a class. French. It's sort of funny. I never tried to learn French all the time Jean-Claude and I were living together, but now . . ."

"I read that piece of yours on grasshoppers in the paper. I thought it was first-rate."

"I guess even grasshoppers should have their day. How nice of you to say so!"

"I'm reading a lot. I have plenty of free time since I quit work."

"Looking around for something different?"

"Jean-Claude said I should stop waiting on tables and stay home and read. So I do."

"I see."

"He said I should use my I.Q."

"He must respect you very much."

"I get a little antsy sometimes. I'm sort of the active type."

"So Jean-Claude told me."

"Oh?"

"It was all complimentary."

"Yes, Jean-Claude is very sweet to me, I must admit."

"And you're sweet back to him . . ."

"Did he say I wasn't?"

"He hasn't said anything to me. He seldom calls."

"*Ahhh!*" There was the sound of a swallow. "*Pardonnez-moi!* Sorry, I'm drinking a strawberry milk shake."

"Sounds delicious," I said.

"Want some?"

"Over the phone?"

There was a split-second beat from Dennis. "I could bring it over, I suppose."

"Ah, but you don't know where I live."

"On Bay Street. I saw it in Jean-Claude's address book. You won't tell him I peeked, will you?"

"When do I ever see him?"

"He's very possessive about certain things. I guess I'm a little mad at him right now."

"Those things don't matter, Dennis. At least you have him."

"Oh, he's very generous with me. It's not that I'm complaining. But he threw a royal fit because I ripped one of his dirty old slippers."

My heart waited. "I guess he's had those a long time."

"It was an accident."

"None of those things matter. Believe me."

"Oh, I *know!* But you know how hard it is to tell Jean-Claude off face to face."

"He does have some sort of power, doesn't he?"

"He sits me down on the couch, then looks me right in the eye like a bullet and gives me a list of six things I'm doing wrong."

"He used to do the same to me."

"And you didn't resent it?"

"At the time I did. Not now."

"I don't really want to be smothered . . . even by someone as wonderful as Jean-Claude."

I could hear him finish off the milk shake, and I imagined the strawberry foam on his lips. I couldn't put my finger on it exactly, but Dennis suddenly struck me as crude.

"Well, what were we talking about?" he said.

I had an idea, like a long, cold pin in my brain. "You and me, I think," I said.

"That sounds interesting," he smiled over the phone.

"Perhaps we could have lunch one day."

"Or dinner," he said.

"Or dinner, right."

"Have you had dinner tonight?"

I paused. "As a matter of fact I haven't."

"Are you free?"

"Sure, but . . . haven't you eaten already?"

"Only dessert . . . Besides, I like *two* desserts sometimes," Dennis said.

"I have asked you both here to discuss our life," Jean-Claude said. He picked up a magazine that Dennis had probably left on the chair, and signalled for me and Dennis to sit down.

I looked at the triangle we made—Dennis in denim coveralls and white socks, some sunburn on his young face, from the beach where we'd been the day before; Jean-Claude in old work clothes, looking nervous and overextended. He was quite short, I noticed, five-six at most. It was funny—he didn't seem short. He hitched up the knees of his work pants and sat down. I'd worn a suit coat, to hide the perspiration I knew would pour down my sleeves.

"Aren't you going to serve a beverage while you have your scene?" Dennis said.

Jean-Claude returned a brutal look and sat forward on the edge of the sofa. "Have you two been seeing each other?"

"Well, I—" I started. How courageous to risk his emotions like this, I thought.

Dennis chuckled. "Come on, Jean-Claude! We're big boys now."

Jean-Claude ignored him and stared at me.

Dennis and I exchanged glances. We had seen each other about a dozen times.

"I do *not* intend to make a fool of myself!" Jean-Claude went on, playing with the edges of the magazines he'd stacked on the coffee table.

Dennis squirmed and pulled on the bib of his coveralls. "Is this all necessary?"

"What do you expect!" Jean-Claude almost snarled. "Sneaking behind my back!"

"Would you prefer that we did it in front of you?" Dennis said, and I gritted my teeth at the unkindness.

Jean-Claude suddenly looked vulnerable. A shadow filled his eyes, and he seemed short of breath. I wanted to go over and stroke his body, but I sat still. All he said was, "Dennis . . .?"

"Oh, this is so boring!" Dennis said. "Trying to call me on the carpet because I'm having sex with someone else!" He acknowledged me with a nod. "Someone who's very good sex, by the way."

I nodded back. So Dennis had noticed. Good, I'd worked hard enough at it.

"And what do *you* say?" Jean-Claude asked me. "Why are you so silent?"

"Maybe we can work out some solution," I said, drying my forehead with my coat sleeve.

Jean-Claude's eyes drove right through mine. "I suppose you would like to move back in. To sleep three in a bed!" he said.

You know I still want you, don't you? I answered with my eyes. And you don't want me, do you? Do you?

"If you're not careful I may move in with Will!" Dennis snapped.

Jean-Claude looked stricken. "You would not do this, would you?"

"Look, I'm not trying to be a manipulating bastard, so please don't force me into that role! We have a free-and-easy thing going together, and when it stops being free-and-easy, maybe it's time to cancel it."

"But I love you!" Jean-Claude said, and I felt the sweat under my arms chill my skin.

"That's very nice," Dennis said. "I'm glad. But you can't chain me in this house, Jean-Claude!"

"I'm nice to you! I give you things—"

The sight of Jean-Claude itemizing the advantages on his fingers made me sick to my stomach. I looked at the wall.

"It was just an arrangement!" Dennis said. "Do you think I like being treated like a kept boy?"

"I've never done this for *anyone else*," Jean-Claude said, blinking. "For no one else!"

I wanted to leave the room. The sweat was ice under my arms now.

"Maybe it's time I made a move," Dennis said. "I'm twenty-eight years old!" he looked at me.

"You don't want to live with *Will!*" Jean-Claude said. "You are not serious!"

"We haven't even talked about it. But you're forcing the issue," Dennis said, looking anguished.

I said nothing and wouldn't meet Dennis' gaze. No, I didn't want to live with him.

"We'll just have to see what works out," Dennis said.

"But *Will?* How can you love *Will.*"

Don't say any more, Jean-Claude, I whispered in my skull. Please.

He gestured at me dismissively. "He will not be a good lover for you, Dennis. He is never satisfied. You don't even know him!"

"Jean-Claude—" I said.

"It's true!" he spat at me. "You were a lazy lover, did you know that?"

"Jean-Claude!"

"You did not *love* me!" Jean-Claude shouted. "I was a machine to make love to *you!* You think I didn't know? You wanted lazy, home sex! Convenient sex! That's what you gave me. Easy, easy sex—that's what I was to you! I do not call that *love!*" His voice broke and I shivered.

The shivers melted in the acid in the center of my body . . . He was right. I hadn't loved him until he'd stopped loving me.

"Hmm, that was good!" Dennis said, scratching my stomach. He stretched and yawned in the bedclothes, then snuggled up next to me. I stroked his cheek.

"Yes, very agreeable," I said.

"You're always so cool, Will. I don't think I've ever seen you lose control."

I patted his cheek twice. "That's the secret of my charm," I smiled.

"Hey, what's the time?"

I picked up my watch from the nightstand, leaning. "Ten-thirty."

"I guess we're safe. Jean-Claude said he wouldn't be

home till after eleven."

I looked at the woodcuts on the wall, at Jean-Claude's blue robe hanging on the clothes tree in the corner. "He usually keeps his promises," I said.

"Wonder what the old boy would do if he caught us in his bed?"

"Nothing melodramatic, probably. He loves you too much."

Dennis put his leg over mine. "Yeah, and I don't know why he does either." He gave a big, open-mouthed yawn, then said, "Sometimes I think it would be best if I just moved out and left him."

My belly felt like there was a lighted match inside. "Oh, don't do that," I said.

"Why not? Aren't you a *little* jealous at least? He and I still have sex occasionally, you know."

I put the top back on the poppers. "I know."

"Aren't you outraged?" Dennis was grinning, but I could tell he wanted me to say something loving.

In answer I ran my knuckles down his spine.

"Ouch!"

"You love it. Admit it."

"Not that hard."

I lay on top of him, pinning his wrists on the pillows. "What're you going to do about it?"

"Will!" he said, half laughing, writhing, but not very hard.

"I give you what you want, don't I?" I said staring down into his handsome face. His teeth were like symmetrical fragments of frost.

Dennis kissed up at me. "Hey, I love you," he said.

"Thank you."

"Do you want me to stop seeing Jean-Claude—for good?"

"It isn't necessary to do that." I thought of Jean-Claude, whom I hadn't seen for months—the solid, small body that I used to hold, the way he used to stroke the bridge of my nose, his cock entering me. I felt a wave of yearning like an addict's for morphine.

Dennis, lying below me, cocked his eye. "I have a question I've been harboring."

"What's that?"

"Did you take up with me on the rebound?"

"No."

"Didn't you at least start having sex with me in order to get back at Jean-Claude?"

"What makes you think that?"

"I'm perceptive, that's why."

"You are—about many, many things," I said.

"Well, *didn't* you? I mean, before you started to fall in love with me."

"No, Dennis, not quite." I hushed him with a kiss between the eyes.

"I'll leave him if you want me to," Dennis offered, his eyes brimming. "I will!"

"We'll see, *mon p'tit lapin*," I said, licking his nipples . . . until he shivered.

But you must never leave Jean-Claude, I whispered inside my body. Never. You're as close as I'll ever get to him, my darling.

human warmth

"My brother thinks I ought to see a psychiatrist," Kerry said. "Think I should?"

"I thought you were happy. Don't spoil my illusion," Roger said.

"I thought I was, but maybe I'm not." Kerry was sitting on the top step inside the back room of the Jackal Bookstore, his muscular back to the wall. Roger, standing below, was looking at him with longing.

"What is happiness anyway—unless it's a hot fuck on a cold night," Roger said, making himself shiver. He was wearing paint-spattered shorts and an old red shirt with the white stitching coming loose on the pockets. He was overweight and lardy and hard-of-hearing and usually slouched. "You don't happen to need some fat in your diet, do you?" he said, grabbing his waist.

"You're not *that* fat, Roger."

"You aren't one of those chubby-chasers I'm always hearing about but never seeing, are you?" He touched his hearing aid. "Come on, speak up, sonny!"

Roger, don't make me hurt you by refusing! Please don't!

"My brother says I'm going to be very unhappy because I won't have a family."

Roger flicked his tongue. "*I'll* be your family."

Kerry shifted on the steps, closing his legs so that his crotch wouldn't show. He'd liked talking with Roger the couple of times he'd seen him in the Jackal, but he could never make it sexually with him. Roger had let himself go—with sloppy fat all through his chest and stomach; big, chunky thighs, even an extra hole cut in his belt for some recent pounds. *Roger, I like you, but your body, your poor body!* "You ever been to a shrink, Roger?" he changed the subject.

"One time, but it didn't work out, as they say. He wasn't my type."

"Sometimes I feel like I'm standing off to the side of my life and everybody else is deciding whether what I do is okay or not. It's bizarre!"

"Sometimes I feel the same way about sex. I'm standing off to the side, watching everybody else do it. I can't remember the last time anybody made a pass at me—even in here in the dark. As soon as they touch my ample body, they depart for leaner pastures. I don't suppose that happens to you, does it? Not with—may I describe you? Not with those eyes—one earthy brown and one heavenly blue, that clipped black beard without a single bare patch in it, and your hammer-hard body like a Roman galley slave's. You even have a big bulge under those jeans."

Kerry didn't know what to say and felt like clearing his throat. He pressed on. "Here I thought we were making progress and now I find my very own brother with all these awful antigay feelings. I told him about coming here to the Jackal for sex—and he tried to be cool, but I could tell he wasn't."

Roger picked a piece of old sleep from his eye and examined it. "Get him a card. He'll change his mind."

"What really got to him was when I said sometimes I have sex with several guys at a time." Kerry gestured toward the orgy rooms at the top of the stairs.

"He'd do it with twenty-two-and-a-half women if he got the chance. It's just envy."

"Think so?" Kerry got up, and his cock made a bulge on his left thigh, and Roger's eyes continued to stare at it.

"It's fascism, Kerry, that's all. They want total conformity!"

"Yeah, sometimes I feel my brother wouldn't mind seeing me in a concentration camp." Kerry pushed the walls on either side of the narrow staircase, then banged them twice.

Roger bent his head forward and almost sighed. "Jesus in Hell, I get so sick and tired of feeling *sorry* for myself! I'd sure love to try something new! I'd like to die of a coronary from having too much sex!"

"I was trying to tell my brother that fucking and sucking are pretty nice activities—with men, I mean. But he said I was being gross." Kerry's brown eye looked almost closed. *Maybe I shouldn't talk about sex at all with you, Roger, I don't mean to lead you on.*

"Hasn't your brother ever sucked a cock?"

"Don't think so . . . but I sucked him once or twice when we were kids."

Roger sat up straighter. "Your own brother?"

Roger, let me out of this, please! Let's just be friends! Damn it, there aren't that many guys a person can just talk to! "He seemed to like it at the time, but he's never referred to it—not for years."

"Homosexual incest! Makes one positively shudder! No wonder he's so 'moral' these days!"

"I sometimes wonder what my brother does in bed now."

"Puts it in his wife's ear. But *that's* okay—it's a heterosexual ear."

"My brother's not a bad guy, you know. He's been very good to me. He paid my way through college and—"

"And out of gratitude you're supposed to deprive the gay world of your delicious private parts and turn them over to your family."

"Excuse me!" Kerry felt something itching and turned his back and removed a piece of lint from his belly button. "That's what's been tickling me. I thought maybe I had crabs."

"You don't have to be so modest and turn away."

I don't want to be a tease, Roger. I ought to leave before this turns ugly.

"You're so gorgeous. Do you work out every day?"

"I don't have to do very much . . . Well, I'd better be—"

Suddenly Roger sighed. "You're gorgeous and you don't have to exercise or anything. I hate you!" He grinned.

"Don't you work out?"

Roger looked down at his flabby body. "You don't do anything—and you look like you sprang from Jupiter's forehead. *I* don't do anything and look like I sprang from his asshole."

"But you're smarter than me," Kerry said sincerely.

Roger bowed from the waist. "You're even *nice!* Oh, how loathsome can one person get!"

Kerry smiled back. "Beauty is only skin deep, they say."

"Who the hell are 'they'?"

"It's true," Kerry said, glancing at himself in the small mirror over the washup sink. *It's not true, appearance is important to both of us. Maybe it shouldn't be, but it is! It simply is!* "We care too much about the flesh, Roger. We really do!"

Roger was still staring at Kerry's crotch. "It makes guys feel good just to drool over you, you know that?"

"What about my *mind*, Roger?" Kerry grinned.

"Okay, you're warm and personable besides being a hunk. Come here!" He held out his arms playfully. "Let me make you happy!"

Kerry didn't quite blush, but he did look down at the floor. "Sometimes I get tired of being 'nice,' you know that? I'd like to be a real bastard sometimes."

"Do you repress yourself? Now *that's* interesting."

"Maybe I should see a shrink about that, huh? Holding back."

Roger poked a fat finger into his own fat thigh several times, leaving a white mark. "If we didn't all hold back, my charming friend, perhaps it would be the end of civilization."

"Do you hold back, Roger?"

"Other people do it for me." He looked directly into Kerry's eyes, without apology. The eyes were a fragile blue. "Know what? There are days when I want to kill."

"Kill who?"

"Oh, psychiatrists. Brothers too smug about their sex drive. People waiting in line at the post office."

"Why them?"

Roger's face went humorless. "The folks who live in terror that their kiddies won't grow up to be straight assholes just like them. I hate them and think they should be dead!"

Kerry felt chilled at the pain in Roger's words. "They hate

us too and think we should be dead."

"Then, damn it, let it come to a war. I'm fed up with one step forward, two steps back!"

"You win more flies with honey than with vinegar, they say."

"So who wants flies?" Roger said.

"If only to swat 'em."

"That's what I'd like to do—get a great big flyswatter and smack their guts into mush!"

"We can't kill everybody we don't like, Roger."

"It's time we turned the hatred around."

"I've never seen you so mad before."

"Excuse me, I'll switch on my winning smile any minute now." Roger showed his tobacco-stained teeth in an exaggerated grin. "Come here, big boy, and we'll forget our troubles *together!*"

"Maybe I'm a rotten lay, Roger."

"I'm willing to risk it."

No, Roger, no! I don't want to go any further with this! I can't cope with your ugliness and your anger and my anger and all the rest of it. He looked at Roger's eyes again. *Yes, your eyes are attractive. If only your eyes were enough.* "I don't seem to be able to get as mad as you do," he heard himself say.

"Because you're not as homely! I have to fight like a goddamned badger to get the little sex I do get, and then some asshole brother like yours wants to send me to a shrink because I get five minutes' worth every other decade!"

Are you threatening me into having sex with you? Or am I imagining it? "What can we do about it?"

"Demand that God send a plague on the straights. A fungus on their tubes or something."

Kerry grinned, somewhat relieved.

"Goddamn it, you're handsome!" Roger said. "Why don't I have a lover like you?"

"You wouldn't like me. I'm sort of messy around the house."

"I'll clean up after you."

"Thanks for the offer, Roger."

"You mean you're considering it?"

"You really wouldn't want me. I have these odd hours where I work. A split shift."

"I can live with a split shift."

"And I come home with my arms all covered with yoghurt."

"I could lick it off."

Am I flirting with him and don't even know it? Should I say goodbye and walk out the door? "I guess I should've majored in yoghurt dipping when I went to college."

"Ah, I spy some bitterness among all that sweetness, Kerry."

Kerry looked up. "I can't find a decent job."

"Isn't dipping yoghurt decent?"

"I'm too old to be doing that now."

"Oh, we'll have a war in a few years and improve the economy."

"Cynic!"

Roger raised his eyebrows. "Since when is telling the plain truth cynical?"

"Maybe so. Maybe in twenty years or so, even my brother will have changed his mind about gays."

"And the next generation can look back on the present troubles with nostalgia." Roger suddenly slapped the wall. "I'll be damned if my suffering's going to be somebody else's fucking musical *comedy!*"

"How do we get out of the present in order to make it into the nostalgia of the future, Roger?"

"If you move in with me, the two of us could plan strategy together."

Kerry checked his zipper with a fingertip, to make sure it was fastened. "Roger, you're going to make my head so big I'm going to need a shrink after all."

Roger leaned back against the wall, letting his stomach protrude. "How long is your dick, Kerry?"

"Roger!"

"I've seen it hard in the back room here, but I've never actually measured it myself."

"It's all right."

"Is it nine inches?"

"What difference does it make?"

"The same principle the ancient Greeks or somebody

had. Bigger is better. I'm just trying to be classical."

"Sometimes I wish my dick was smaller."

"That's been my problem too. All these men keep pestering me to sit on it. I have to chase them off with a stick."

Roger is charming when he wants to be. I have to give him that. "Maybe if you lost a little weight, Roger—"

"I like donuts too much, and why bother? I'd just be gorgeous and then everybody would be after me, and I'd be getting VD all the time."

"You'd have to be careful—and selective."

"Let me tell you a moral tale about how selective I was. I didn't have anal sex for *two* solid years because I'd gotten warts the last time. Get the picture—I was a paragon of rectal virtue. But finally, after two years, I went to a so-called 'model'—and he gave me the worst case of anal warts since God invented Mississippi."

"Seriously?"

"I swear on a stack of Korans."

"I've never had anything except the clap once. I guess I'm pretty lucky."

"Do you like to get fucked?" Roger looked up daringly, a puckish expression on his face. "You can confide in me."

Kerry felt the smile cracking on his own face. *I'm getting in too deep*, he told himself. "It's been known to happen," he answered.

"How old are you?"

"Twenty-nine."

"I'm forty-three." Roger slumped on the bottom step in mock despair, his shirt stretching away from the buttons because of the fat chest. His hand lay a couple of steps closer to Kerry.

"Roger, do you mind if I say something?" He stood up, supporting himself with both hands on the low-hanging ceiling.

Roger looked up the stairs, at Kerry's crotch above him. "Speak up, sonny!" He cupped his ear.

"I'd like to say something."

"Shoot."

"I don't mean to preach because I don't really know you that well."

"Want to come back to my place and give me a whole sermon?" Roger's hand moved up another step.

Kerry grinned instead of saying what he wanted to say. He went down the steps past Roger to the washup sink and grabbed a paper towel and blotted around his mouth. *I don't want to hurt your feelings, but, Roger, I'm not going to have sex with you!* "Have you ever seen a psychiatrist, Roger?" he said aloud.

"Didn't you ask me that earlier?"

"Sorry—I forgot. I guess it's all this pressure my brother's been putting on me." Kerry blotted around his mouth again.

"Drown him."

"He talked about my 'failure of introjection.' "

"What the hell does that mean?"

"I think it means he thinks my sex life stinks."

"Kill him."

"Maybe that's a bit extreme."

"He doesn't mind crushing you with all *his* horseshit!"

"I don't think my brother really knows anything about homosexuality. And those times with me didn't make him tolerant."

"Come on, let's go kill your brother! An army of lovers and all that."

Kerry picked up the bar of soap near the sink and squeezed it till his knuckles turned yellow. "He made me feel like I was 'confessing' something to him, and I haven't felt that way in years."

"Did he say you were afraid of women?"

"Yes."

"I hope you at least said it's *him* that's afraid of men!"

"I didn't think of it."

"See, if *I'd* been with you, we could've handled him!"

The door to the back room buzzed and another man, in washed-out Levi's, came in and squeezed past Kerry and Roger and disappeared up the stairs.

"Nice, huh?" Roger said.

"Mmmm."

"Why don't you follow him? Then I'll follow *you*—and I'll get some lovely leftovers."

It's time I said something. "You make it sort of hard for

61

me to talk to you, Roger," Kerry said.

"I do?"

"Never mind." Kerry smiled and kept back the words. Roger just wasn't sexy and telling him that wouldn't do any good.

"Why is it hard for you to talk to me, Kerry?" Roger sounded a little hurt.

"I wasn't serious."

"We're talking nicely, aren't we?"

"Very nicely."

"Are you holding something back?"

"No."

"Are you madly in love with me? Tell me. I can take it."

"You have a nice sense of humor, Roger."

"Nobody could stand me if I didn't."

Kerry looked into Roger's eyes and could see the years of rejection, the vulnerability. "Are you happy, Roger?"

"Not very."

"Do you suppose gays have more sadness in them?"

"No, *everybody's* miserable! But it becomes a way of life and you hardly notice."

"I wonder if I'm happy."

"Once upon a time there was a handsome Prince who had everything going for him—looks, sex appeal, youth, sincerity, you name it. And this Prince had his share of good days, considering that he had to contend with tooth decay and scabies like everybody else. But then one day a Wicked Magician came to the castle and told the Prince that he (the Prince) was a failure.

'Why am I a Failure?' asked the Prince.

'Listen, you little punk,' said the Magician, 'everybody in this village has to pass the goddamn Oedipal Exam! Every goddamned body! Get it?'

'Gee, I feel bad,' said the Prince.

'Well, I should hope so!' said the Wicked Magician. 'What you need is a good case of Depression—serves you right for being so independent, you little shithead!' "

Roger stopped.

"And what happened to the Prince?" Kerry asked.

"In some versions he marries the Magician's daughter

and buys a bungalow in the suburbs. In the updated version, the Prince stuffs the Wicked Magician into an oven, marries the frog, and lives happily ever after."

"I don't know . . . I don't know," Kerry said flatly. "It's like fighting voodoo. Where do you begin?"

"You're supposed to ask where the frog came from."

"Okay. Where?"

Roger made a croaking noise. "Nice, huh? Kiss me!"

"Very nice." Kerry pushed on. "Maybe I should remind my brother we had sex together."

"A lot of them think they can't be 'real men' and like cock too. And when you point out the fallacy in their thinking, they beat you up."

"Nobody's going to beat me up," Kerry said softly.

"Don't get too butch now, or you'll wind up acting just like the enemy."

"What am I supposed to do—let 'em call me names and smack me around too? You keep saying, 'Let's go kill 'em!' But I don't see you actually *doing* anything!"

Roger looked down at his big legs. "I don't know why we don't resort to violence very often. It's very bad for our image—nobody takes a sissy seriously."

"I wonder what would happen if we started knocking over desks in psychiatrists' offices. Or punching out anybody who says bad things about us."

"Like the blacks do, you mean?"

"Yeah."

Roger shrugged. "People still say things behind their backs."

"They don't force them to change their color, though. That's something."

"They love to shoot niggers when they riot. How do you think they'd feel about the queers?"

"Just a few minutes ago you were goading me into the streets—and now you're talking me out of it."

"That's how we fags are. Fickle, fickle."

Kerry glanced over at Roger's impish smile. "Fuck you!"

"As your psychiatrist, I find ziss indulgence in this homo-flesh repulzive, anti-zocial, and certainly zee most exciting thing in my whole humdrum day!"

Kerry kicked the bottom step. "I wonder what it would be like to be gay and have nobody try to change me or be snide—I wonder if we'll ever get to that stage, where we can just see what being gay all by itself is like, without all, all the—"

"Jungian, Adlerian, Behaviorist, Primal Screamian, Aesthetic Realtian, you-name-it shit!"

"Just me and life."

"Well, straights seem to have *their* problems, so don't expect too much."

"Defeatist."

"Unless, of course, you move in with me, Kerry. I can see us now—a nonsexist, nonroleplaying, noncompetitive relationship that would make the world take note. Kiss me."

"Would it work out, Roger?"

"We'd have long talks and go to Cultural Events and make love with the lights on."

"But would it last?"

"You never know until you start."

Kerry looked at Roger's unappetizing body, the cheesy skin, the hearing aid, the lips like two wet bugs. "I'm not ready to settle down yet, Roger."

"Will you keep me on your list of eligibles? I may not be attractive, but you can be sure as hell I'd be faithful."

Poor Roger, Kerry thought. *But he doesn't want my pity. I'm just putting him down if I think this way.*

"I'll lose weight for you," Roger said, mocking himself.

"Lose weight for yourself, Roger."

Roger winced. "*Touché!*"

"I didn't mean it sarcastically. I'm sorry."

"Were you ever a Boy Scout, Kerry?"

"Yes, why?"

"You seem like the type. Let me see—you grew up in Minnesota on a dairy farm."

"It was Wisconsin, and my dad ran a hotel."

"Same thing. And you were president of the senior class and voted Most Likely to Succeed."

"Most-All-Around Boy."

"Really? That's delightful!"

"And what about *your* past, Roger?"

"Not worth discussing."

"Sounds intriguing."

"Let me finish your biography. Your asshole brother belongs to the Methodist Church in Tiburon and sends his kids to a school with high tuition."

"And assumes that he's the absolute center of the universe."

"And everybody else is a Deviant from the Norm. His Norm. Is his name Norman by any chance?"

"Alan."

"I've always hated that name. Don't you really *hate* him?"

"Not hate. He just gets under my skin sometimes."

"I'd like to get under your skin sometime, Kerry." He winked. "What are you into? S&M? B&D?"

"Hugging and kissing."

"Sounds wild."

"And what are you into, Roger?" Kerry regretted the question being dragged out of him. Roger would misunderstand.

"I could surprise you. When I get in bed, I take off this fat suit I'm wearing—and I become a handsome gladiator."

"A fat suit?"

"You've got to believe, Kerry, or you're going to grow up to be a bitter old man. We're all just wearing fat suits or ugly suits, and all we need is a kiss to make us take them off."

Kerry looked at Roger's ugly face and the hearing-aid that seemed like a growth on his ear. *Would it be wise to kiss Roger? Just a kiss and nothing more? Or would that just be cock-teasing him?*

"You've grown silent, Kerry, or is it just my hearing?"

"I was just thinking what my brother would say about something."

"What's that?"

Kerry touched the corner of his mouth nervously. "Kissing a man."

Roger looked up. "Anybody I know?"

"I'm wondering what my brother would say about somebody who just wants to kiss somebody . . ."

"Just kiss?"

"Yeah." Kerry felt embarrassed, the back of his shirt growing damp.

"Can a kiss exist in a vacuum?" Roger shook his head.

"See how I am, Kerry! I don't even have the *kiss* yet and already I'm asking for more."

"I'd like to kiss you, Roger."

"But nothing more . . ." Roger smiled valiantly. "I understand."

"It's turning sour as we talk about it."

"Not that sour." Roger smiled.

"I'd like to kiss you because you've helped me talk about my brother and because gays have got to stick together and because people are so nasty to each other and . . ."

"French kiss or plain?"

"Which do you prefer?"

Roger thought for a second. "Plain, I think."

"You're nice." Kerry stepped over and tried to put his arms around Roger, who was sitting on the bottom step, but the angle made it awkward.

"Should I stand up?" Roger asked.

In answer Kerry brought his lips close to the other man's and then held Roger's face with both hands. He held the kiss for more than a minute. Two of the men who were cruising in the room above glanced down at them, then moved on. Kerry kept his mouth pressed hard against Roger's lips, aware that it was artificial, that it was a gesture. Roger's eyes were closed.

It was Roger who moved away. "Thank you, Kerry."

"I'm sorry it wasn't better."

Roger rubbed his lower lip, to touch where the kiss had been. "In this valley of travail, it was something . . . I'm not complaining."

"If only a kiss could make it all better."

"Hey, do you think maybe the French one would've led to something *more* between us?" He almost smiled, still touching his lip.

Kerry pushed open the door and looked back and waved before he left, something tight and sour in his stomach. *Why do we have to be the way we are?* he thought.

victor

Were those voices? Were they his students? Why didn't they come in then? Were they arguing or conspiring or something? Had one of them sneaked a look through the window? He waited, uncomfortble, his "office" hour after class about up.

Victor was Jewish on his father's side, and embarrassed; he was also gay, and afraid; he looked like Porky Pig besides. Sometimes he told himself that his little arms and legs didn't matter, nor did his porkchop coloring. At other times he told himself that his arched nostrils and slanting eyes made him look sexy, like a Mongolian, an almost blond Mongolian. He'd strike a warrior pose like a member of Genghis Khan's hordes and believe for a few moments that he was a Tartar, as ruthless and savage as the ancestor who'd probably raped one of his great-great-great-great grandmothers. Then the moment would pass and he'd say to himself that he looked more like tartar sauce. Didn't tartar sauce go with porkchops? No? Well, it went with fish.

It was time to leave. Nobody seemed to be coming to talk with him after twenty minutes, although somebody was still outside the classroom. He removed his flowery tie and stuffed it into his briefcase sitting on the desk. Then he went over and straightened one of the desks a student had jostled in his hurry to leave when class had ended. Victor bent down and picked up a scrap of paper, for there'd been a nasty warning from the high school principal, who allowed Victor's extension university to use the rooms at night. Some students had left Coke bottles and cigarette stubs in the classroom next door, and Dr. Monasch, the director of the program, had issued a notice to all instructors that classes might be cancelled unless the violations ceased.

He gave the classroom a final check, preparing to douse the lights and go out into the sultry Okinawan evening. He thought about taking off his suit jacket, as he had his tie, but he was afraid that someone from the local Education Office might report him to Dr. Monasch. Rules were strict about wearing a coat and tie when teaching. Under both arms there was oily sweat, and he supposed his jacket smelled bad—but he needed this job, needed it desperately, and so he left the jacket on. Indeed he was scrupulous about all the regulations, the forms he was required to fill out, careful not to say anything in class about religion or politics or sex—certainly not his own kind of sex—or about the military itself; he even spent extra time with his worst students, tutoring them about fundamentals like what a verb was. He didn't mind the extra time involved, even though it was shocking how awful so many of the students were. Supposedly they were taking college English, and yet some of them could barely read, could barely write a sentence. Some couldn't do that! They were far worse than the students he'd had back in Oregon. When he coached them privately —though they became more human—he discovered that they talked exactly the way they wrote. Still, he told himself, he was uplifting them. He hoped he'd "saved" any number from D's and F's because of the extra help he'd given them. As it was, he felt terrible about having to give so many low grades. Sometimes he agonized over a D for several hours, changing the grade in his gradebook back and forth ten or twelve times. *But this is a university!* he would say, if he finally decided to give the student the lower grade. *What does a "university" mean? I'm giving this sergeant a C-minus when he can't even understand what our essays are saying!*

Victor stood with his thumb over the light switch, not wanting to leave. It would be hotter in his own room; he didn't have an air-conditioner, and even though the one in the classroom tonight had been defective, its hum seeming to make the students drowsier than usual, it was still cooler in the classroom than in the room where he lived.

He thought about Alaska. Maybe he should go to Alaska! He'd gotten as far as Okinawa, after being let go when his small college in Oregon had reduced its staff. If he could just get some cash together—it would be cool there, perhaps even cold, no Dr. Monasches issuing demands and forms, no hot little rooms off base, no large classes of freshman composition. If only he could get away from Okinawa, from this extension course he was teaching! Four more weeks before the term ended, then one more term after that! He calculated the number of class meetings, the number of compositions he'd have to mark before summer school. Of course he knew that he'd really have to teach summer school as well, to get a few dollars ahead.

He wondered if he should go back and finish his Ph.D. But the idea filled him with lassitude. He was forty-one now, too old to go back to school. And even the Ph.D.'s were having difficulty. Dr. Monasch had told Victor he was lucky to be getting courses, since the university had turned down the applications of six Ph.D's in one month. Victor had nodded, holding his part-timer's contract in his hands carefully. The $675 for the eight weeks would come in handy. More than handy—absolutely necessary. He remembered Dr. Monasch's unattractive eyes perusing the grade sheet, then the man saying, "No A's this term, Mr. Kepko? And only three B's?" He hadn't said any more than that. Just an unsubtle hint that Victor was too hard a grader. "I always like to think that our students are under a special hardship, being in the military and working long hours and all." Dr. Monasch had smiled, a grim smile that told Victor he'd better watch himself.

"If I could only get away! If I only had some money!" he whispered aloud, flipping out the light and standing in the darkness. He opened the classroom door and stared at a few students who were standing outside, smoking. He couldn't see their faces very well in the dark, but he thought they were black. Victor snapped the lock on the door.

"You got a minute, Mr. Kepko?" a voice said.

Victor waited, as one of the group approached. It was Miss Washington, the black WAC in his course. She was holding the theme he'd passed back to her that evening. He'd given it an F. "Why, yes, Miss Washington," he said.

69

She flicked her cigarette away into the grass. She was wearing fatigues—jungle fatigues, he thought they were called, with a camouflage pattern on them. She was short and bulky and unfeminine. He wondered if she might be a lesbian. She always wore fatigues to class.

"I wants to talk with you about my theme, but I've been waiting to see," she explained.

"Certainly." He looked over at the three other forms in the darkness, two of them male. Were they waiting for her? "Do you want to go back into the classroom?"

"Yeah." Miss Washington turned to the others. "Wait here for me, all right?" They muttered something that Victor couldn't understand.

Suddenly Victor remembered. "Oh, I'm sorry. I don't have a key." He tried the lock again to be sure. "Can it wait till next time?"

"I'd like to talk to you tonight—if you don't mind." There was more demand than request in her tone. The WAC had crumpled the theme, Victor could tell, and then smoothed it out.

He tried to see the other three persons. "Are they in our class too?" He pointed. "Do they wish to discuss their themes?"

"No, they's just friends of mine. They's not in your class."

Victor felt vaguely alarmed. All during the class period Miss Washington had refused to look at him after he'd passed back the themes and they'd discussed them.

"We could go down nearer the parking lot, if you like," he suggested. "There's more light there."

"Sure." She followed him along the sidewalk until they got to the high school's main parking lot.

He spotted a wooden bench with many initials carved into it and sat down and gestured for the girl to be seated too. "Now, what seems to be the problem?"

Miss Washington didn't sit. Instead she flapped the paper back and forth like a fan, but she wasn't fanning herself. "This here's the *third* one you put a flag on!" she said belligerently. In the light he could see her short, tufted hair, the broad nose, the lip she was gnawing. There was an air of street-wisdom about the girl.

"Is it the third?" Victor said politely. "You didn't turn in the second paper," he added, hinting that she might have four F's now if she had.

"I was sick," she said immediately.

"You should've mentioned it to me, don't you think?" He knew that she was a hopeless student, almost illiterate. He'd read her themes with pain because Miss Washington was so obviously a failure. He bent over backwards for black students, feeling that they'd encountered special difficulties in their homes, in their schooling. He was giving Mr. Rodgers in the same class a C-minus even though he didn't deserve it. But with Miss Washington's themes there was nothing else Victor could do but fail them.

"You got something *personal* against me?" she asked, putting her foot up on the bench, not far from his knee.

"Personal?" He felt his throat catch. "What do you mean by that?"

"Something personal!" She waved the corrected theme toward him, and he could see his red marks like bloodstains on the paper.

"Why in the world would I have anything personal against you, Miss Washington? I don't even know *whose* essays I'm reading until after I put the grade on them. That's why I have you put your name on the back."

"You sure put this flag here real easy-like." She made some sort of deprecating sound with her lips.

"I have nothing personal against you!" he answered, with a bit more volume. "I grade each paper in light of the assignment and in light of standards of college composition."

"It couldn't be because I'm black maybe, could it?" She knew she was pushing him and didn't meet his eye.

"How dare you," he said clearly, looking over toward the girl's friends who were waiting for her in the shadows. "Are you accusing me of prejudice?"

"I didn't say nothing 'bout that. All I says is that you flunk my papers real easy."

He knew his voice was rising in pitch. "Perhaps you overestimate your abilities." He'd heard his voice once on a tape-recorder; it seemed high and breathy.

She snorted. "Who says? You? I showed this paper to a *professor*, and he say it was good!"

He wanted to stand up so they'd be on eye level, but he

forced himself to remain on the bench, quieting his voice as well. "What professor?"

"A professor I knows!" She was airy with contempt now, having made her move. "A professor of English and math!"

He paused, then said, "A unique combination for a professor."

"Well, *he* like it, even you didn't!"

Victor placed his hand on his briefcase, for something to touch. "Did he? Did he help you write it?"

"No, he didn't! I wrote it myself!" She was so insistent Victor suspected she had had help from somebody. Her last theme *had* been somewhat improved, if still hopeless with errors, with confused thinking. It was in her hand now, being shaken in his direction.

"Did you revise the theme before you turned it in?" he asked.

"I worked on it a long, long time!" She was picking at the wood of the bench, splintering it.

Suddenly Victor felt weary, useless. He looked up at the girl standing above him, then past her at the stars. They were trivial and faraway. He could feel the weight of the weather and he had to sit forward on the vandalized bench so that his feet would touch the ground. What was the use of everything? he wondered. What was the use of anything! Miss Washington with her absurd theme! Teaching bored and boring remedial students in Okinawa on a U.S. military base, eking out a living on a minimal salary! Here he was talking to Miss Washington about whether she'd revised her theme once or twice. It would be a waste no matter how many times she rewrote it. He felt desperately sorry for her. She had overly thick lips and spoke ghettoese and didn't have two brains in her head, and he felt guilty about failing her. She was a slave, a descendant of slaves, but still a slave, a tough, stupid girl from Chicago or someplace, in the Army now and struggling for the American Dream, encouraged because she was black, because she was a woman. Opportunities were opening up for her now, and he was going to fail her, and burn her dream, because she was stupid and illiterate. It made him sick. And it was so *damned* hot, a dense tropical heat that infiltrated the body like a disease!

So hot he could see the sweat on Miss Washington's upper lip as she flipped open the theme to the second page.

"What's you mean by this?" She tapped at some comment he'd made.

He stood up to examine the paper with her, looking where she pointed. The sentence she'd written was: "With the changeing fact of America and in the mist of all dierties, todays women is taking her neutral place in her new life style." He closed his eyes, wondering what to say to her. "My comment is that 'neutral' is not the word you mean here. Maybe you mean 'natural.' " He didn't feel he could tell her more, going over the dozens of corrections in the semidarkness.

"I think it sound good!" Miss Washington argued.

"And the singular of 'women' is 'woman.' Or else the verb should be 'are.' That's 8A in our text, remember? We discussed it last Thursday."

"Yeah," she conceded.

What was the use of it all! He ached inside. He could stand there all night long and not change the girl. It was too late, too late! He had eight weeks in a term to eradicate the patterns of a lifetime—not reading, not writing, not studying. It was absurd! It was 8A in the text! He might as well be telling an Eskimo. It was sad and pathetic and horrible, but he wasn't responsible for racial prejudice; it wasn't his fault that Miss Washington's ancestors had been auctioned off on blocks at slave markets, not his fault! And yet here he was stuck with the burden of guilt and responsibility. It wasn't his fault, but he couldn't pass her, no, no, he couldn't pass this girl and hold his head up that he was teaching university courses! Yet it would be so much easier if he simply passed her through—then *she* would like him; so would the Education Center, because then Miss Washington and others like her would enroll on base next term; the Education Center would get its merit points from PACAF, from the number enrolled. And even Dr. Monasch would be happier with Victor; the funds would keep flowing into the university's treasury; the whole process of "education," complete with pious commencement addresses by brigadier generals about our "hard-working students" and all the other crap, would go on unabated! Why didn't Victor just play along, do what they wanted, what was necessary! It would be so much easier, so much, much easier.

"I had a hard life," Miss Washington snapped.

"Am I expected to give you a good grade because you had a hard life?"

"I didn't have no white folks to teach me before!" she said spitefully.

"What do you mean by that?"

"I didn't have no white folks to teach me in high school!" she said more loudly. "Why they got no black men teaching over here?"

He deflected her challenge, feeling them both too intense. "Perhaps you ought to withdraw from the course and wait until a black teacher becomes available, Miss Washington."

"I cain't!" Her eyes were wide and her mouth pouting. "There ain't nobody else on this godforsaken island. That's why I took your course!"

"Well, you aren't writing on a college level. Perhaps you ought to seek remedial help. There's a PREP program here, I believe, mainly for those who want to complete high school—"

"I done did high school!" she said indignantly. "I had a rough life."

"Many of us have rough lives, Miss Washington, but we don't use them as an excuse to get special treatment."

"I'll just *bet* you had a rough life!" she said.

He could feel her hatred as ponderous as the heavy night air. He was getting a headache. "Well, there must be some other program you can enroll in."

"I wants to stay in this class! *This* one! I paid for college!"

"I know! But you obviously aren't going to pass, are you? Wouldn't it be better to try another one?"

"I'm gonna stay in this class and you's gonna read my themes, 'cause *that's* what you get paid for!"

He stepped back from her, surprised at her vehemence. "Now just a minute! You aren't acting very smart, Miss Washington!"

"Don't you call me dumb! I'm not dumb! I can do college!" She was sullen and threatening, her body hunched.

"You're not being very smart psychologically—that's what I meant."

"I'm not dumb!" She sounded almost desperate, and Victor felt pity squeeze inside his chest.

"I'm not saying you're dumb; I'm only saying the way to get what you want is *not* to try to intimidate your teacher! It really isn't!" He wished he could take her in his arms and hug her, let her sob on his shoulder, let them both cry, let them weep fat, wracking tears until both were exhausted. Let it clear the air between them, between the races, the way it did in television programs. A half hour of disagreement resolved at the end by an embrace, a handshake, a trustful nod, the way it was on the television programs he sometimes watched in the Recreation Center on base.

"You're sure it's not something personal?" she repeated, tucking the theme into her back pocket, rolled, to let him know that she didn't care about the theme, about him; he was merely an obstacle in her way.

"I resent what you're saying very much, Miss Washington. I want you to know that!"

"I had a sick mother!"

"I'm sorry! I'm truly sorry about your sick mother, about the place where you grew up. But I can't help it! I can't help it, that's all!"

"Maybe the Equal Opportunities Commission would like to know about you!" It was her trump card, and she dealt it rapidly.

He could feel his face scorch. "I think you'd better go, Miss Washington. And take your friends with you!" He gestured at the group loitering over by the classroom. "If you think you can threaten me and get away with it, you've got another think coming!"

"Yeah, they might be interested to know they got a *bigot* on their all-white faculty!"

"You're the bigot, my dear woman! You're the bigot!" He knew he sounded prissy, but he couldn't control himself. "You most certainly had better withdraw from the class now!"

"I'm *not* gonna withdraw, 'cause you's gonna grade my themes fair!" She strode off, then stopped. "Or else I'm gonna kick your ass, you goddamn queer!"

Dr. Monasch had asked him to stop in to see him when he turned his final grades into the main office. Victor sat crookedly, waiting, watching Dr. Monasch's energetic secretaries typing. In a few minutes a handsome colonel in uniform came out of Dr. Monasch's office. The Director and the colonel shook hands cordially.

Then Dr. Monasch looked up before turning back into his office. "Oh, Mr. Kepko! There you are!"

Victor got up and followed the tall, younger man into the office, which was panelled in teakwood. It was almost cold, because the air-conditioning was turned up so high.

"Sit—sit down."

Victor sat, in one of the woolly white chairs that looked like polar bears, sinking into the cushion. "How have you been, Dr. Monasch?" he inquired politely.

"Can't complain. Can't complain at all!" The Director patted his tummy. He was a slimy man, with slushy blue eyes, a colorless complexion, but tall and straight and poised. "Say, what's this I heard about some student complaining about you?" Dr. Monasch sat behind his large desk and placed his slush-laden eyes on Victor's face.

"It was simply a misunderstanding." Victor stopped himself. A "sir" had almost slipped out.

"Didn't some black girl accuse you of unfair grading?"

Victor looked down at his grade sheet, which he would turn in before he left. Instructors had to turn in their grades in person before they got their paychecks. "The girl was mistaken, but everything's cleared up now, fortunately."

Dr. Monasch should have smiled, but didn't. "Not good to hear stories like this, Mr. Kepko. Gives the university a bad reputation."

Victor felt that he was being swallowed up in the white polar bear cushions. "It's all over and done with, Dr. Monasch."

But the Director wasn't about to be put off—obviously he'd set aside a few minutes that morning to "discuss the matter" with Victor. "I understand your student was black."

"That's right."

"We have some mighty upstanding black students in our

program. Wonderful reports on progress." He lifted a fistful of official-looking documents from his desk.

"I'm glad to hear that," Victor said faintly.

"Mighty fine students, mighty fine reports of progress." He waited for Victor to agree with him.

Victor glanced out the window at the Okinawan greenery. Dr. Monasch had a splendid view—of a small gorge, a couple of small hills. It didn't even look hot outside from in here. "Yes," Victor mumbled.

"Speak up, Mr. Kepko. I hope you speak up more loudly than that in your classroom. How will the students ever *hear* you?" The Director tidied the stack of progress reports.

"I'm sorry."

"By the way, there isn't anything in your background that would bias you against some students, is there, Mr. Kepko? Are you from the South?"

Victor bowed his head. "No, there's nothing in my background. No, I'm not from the South."

Dr. Monasch spotted the speck of opposition in Victor. "I mean, we have no room in our academic program for prejudice or bias—we never have and we never will!" He pinned Victor to the woolly chair with a look.

"It was all a misunderstanding. It's all straightened out now."

"Well, splendid! We wouldn't want anything to interfere with your teaching assignment for next term. It's just splendid!" he grinned as he spoke, a combination of slime and intimidation. Victor felt as if someone's rotting hand were doing something obscene to his body; the secretaries typed away enthusiastically outside the office.

"Is that all, Dr. Monasch?" Victor asked wearily.

The Director stood up behind his large desk. "I had a call from the Equal Opportunities people. Not a nice call, not a nice call whatsoever!"

"I'm sorry."

"It could do the university no good, *no* good at all if word got around that we've got bigots on our staff. Bigots about whom there have also been unsavory sexual rumors." The Director looked sternly at Victor. "Do I make myself perfectly clear, Mr. Kepko?"

"Perfectly."

There was a silence, while only the clack of typewriters and the throb of the air-conditioner filled the spacious office.

"Well, I guess I'd better be going," Victor said.

"Is that your grade sheet with you?"

Victor nodded.

"Do you mind if I see it?" Monasch held out his hand, and after a minuscule hesitation, Victor got up and gave it to him, then sat back down. The man's eyes scanned the names and grades appraisingly. "Yes, yes, yes!" Then he looked at the comment on the bottom that Victor had written in the area provided. "Some of the students in this class were satisfactory. Some needed remedial help." Dr. Monasch wrinkled his lean face. "Why, Mr. Kepko, this sounds dissatisfied!" He smiled. "Are you dissatisfied with our educational program over here?"

"No, I'm not dissatisfied."

"Well, I'm so glad to hear that. Because, after all, Mr. Kepko, there're any number of instructors who just love it over here, just love teaching in Asia! That's why *they* remain. And we always prefer to have people who *enjoy* teaching in our classrooms. Wouldn't you feel the same if you were in my place?"

"Perhaps I would, yes."

"Of course you would! We've been mighty pleased with you so far this year. And I, for one, surely hope you'll continue to want to work with us and the military!"

Victor had to look down. If he could just get out of the office, out of the huge white chair, if he just didn't say anything more, then Dr. Monasch would let him teach for at least one more term. In time they'd get rid of him; he could see that. But at least he'd have one more term, maybe two, if he just didn't say anything more.

"What was the name of that black student again?" Dr. Monasch was skimming the grade sheet once more.

"Miss Washington." Victor thought he might be catching a cold from the air-conditioning.

Dr. Monasch found the name. "There she is!" He laid his

finger beside the computer-typed name. "Oh, I see that she earned a C in your course."

Victor stared down at the rug. "That's correct. She improved a lot in the second half."

the myth

He arrived in Hollywood from Des Moines, handsome, shaggy-headed, a bit underweight, sunburned from the summer job in a bus depot washing busses. He'd never had an acting lesson in his life and yet he knew he was going to be a star. Sometimes he actually ached with wanting it as he lay on his single bed in the Los Gatos Hotel, a two-bit firetrap near Hollywood Boulevard. He'd won a prize for playing the lead in *Our Town* in high school, but several friends had scoffed when Ned told them he was going to Hollywood to be in the movies. "In the movies?" they'd asked him, barely hiding their amusement. "You might as well stay here in Des Moines, because very few ever make it there in Tinsel Town."

On the second day in Hollywood Ned got a reading with a producer, and did a scene from *Our Town*. The producer, quite sallow and grumpy, told him to come back a week later, for a second reading.

"Can you ride a horse?" the producer asked him after the second time.

"I can try," Ned said.

"You're supposed to say, 'Hell yes, I ride like the Lone Ranger.'"

Ned thought he'd fouled things up.

"You've got the job," the producer said, "if you join a union."

He acted in a television western for a week, and when he saw the show, all that remained of the scene was a shot of him patting a horse's tail.

But the scene led to his second job.

"I've done a show," he said at his next interview, with a pockmarked female producer who had pencilled-in eyebrows.

"I'm looking for somebody who can run pretty fast. For a documentary about the Olympics."

"I can run pretty fast," Ned said.

"You're skinny enough," she said.

"The camera makes me look heavier," Ned answered.

"Oh, getting to know your way around, eh?" the female producer smirked.

"A little."

"Let me see you run."

"Here?"

"Run in place. I wanna see the way you move."

Ned felt slightly silly, but he ran in place, speeding up at the end, pretending to collapse as he crossed an imaginary finish line.

The pockmarked producer scowled. "I said *run*, not ham it up!"

Ned felt like a fool, his stomach moving in and out.

"But you run pretty good, kid," she said. "It'll only be three days' work."

"That'll be all right."

Now he had two acting jobs to his credit. And he began to wonder if he could get a speaking part. He still didn't have an agent. Everybody told him he should get an agent.

"We know some guy at Fox who's looking for two young types who can fight on a raft. One of them has to fall into some rough water. Can you swim?" the agent said.

"I swam a lot back home."

"Can you swim with a camera watching you?"

"I think I can manage."

"You don't even have to give me a blow job," the agent said. "We like your style, kid—sort of cornball and cute. You ought to do something about your teeth, though. Have you thought about caps?"

"I thought a more natural look was in," Ned said.

"Maybe so," the agent answered. "Just an idea. Is Ned Galveston your real name?"

"Yes."

"I love it."

"Thank you."

"Are you straight, bi, or gay?"

Ned hesitated. "I'm . . . I'm gay."

"You act butch enough. Don't sweat it."

"Are you gay?" Ned asked the agent.

"My little secret, friend."

"Do you think being gay will hurt me?"

"Who knows? Maybe yes, maybe no. Don't get caught in a compromising situation, that's all."

"I promise."

"Can you fuck a woman if you have to?"

"Why?"

"Some of these broads might want stud service now and then. Are you up to that?"

"Nobody's asked for that kind of thing so far."

"Well, you probably don't turn everybody on, friend. Don't let your good looks go to your head—ever. Got it? Got to be more than a piece of meat if you're going to be a star. Pieces of meat we got, believe me."

"I think I can fall off a raft." Ned smiled.

"We want you to come to a party some big director's throwing. Can you make smalltalk and look sexy at the same time?"

"I can try."

"We'll show you around, maybe somebody'll like your style. It's all personal whim around this place."

"I'm game."

The party was held at a sprawling adobe mansion built on two rolling hills in Bel Air, where the host greeted the agent by name, offering champagne.

"This here's our new client, Ned Galveston," the agent said.

"Glad you could come tonight," the director said. He was muscular and pensive and dressed in a sleeveless green silk shirt. "What have you done so far?"

Ned mentioned the two films he'd been in.

"Ned's sort of a cross between a young American Cary Grant and a butch Randolph Scott, don't you think?" the agent said.

"You're such a liar," the director told the agent, good-naturedly. "We'll have to talk later, Ned. I've got some more guests coming." The director nodded and went over to a cluster of handsome people near the spouting fountain.

"Personally, I think his movies stink," the agent said to Ned. "But he's very big right now. Had three smashes in a row."

"I saw his last. I thought it was wonderful," Ned said.

"To each his own."

Ned and the agent ate some canapés and drank champagne, wandering around the huge lawn. Various people spoke to the agent, and Ned was introduced. Everywhere he saw people in handsome, summery clothes, thrilling, important people talking about making movies, actual movies in Hollywood. He even caught a glimpse of a female superstar across the room, splashing some of her champagne at a tall man in a tuxedo.

Ned left the agent and walked toward the swimming pool to get a closer look at the superstar. Yes, it was really she, and she was stuffing orange peels down some woman's neckline, giggling. Blue mermaids and mermen were carved all around the edge of the pool, and Ned pretended to examine the mer-people and watched the superstar at the same time, sipping his champagne and trying to look poised.

"What're you up to?" a voice behind him asked.

It was the muscular director he'd met earlier.

"I was just looking at the decorations. They're very nice."

"How old are you?"

"Twenty."

"I'm forty. Do you want to fuck?"

Ned was surprised at the suddenness. He took a step backward and fell into the swimming pool, and didn't even think to close his mouth.

"You nasty man!" a flamboyant red-wigged woman yelled at the director. "Hey, Burton's pushed somebody into the swimming pool, the brute!" She laughed.

Everybody was laughing, even Ned, as the director knelt down and offered his hand and pulled Ned out of the water.

"Get some towels, please!" the director called to a petite girl serving drinks. She ran over with a handful of serving towels and the director started swabbing Ned's neck and head. "You okay?" he asked.

Ned's nose felt full of chlorine. Even his eyes stung a bit. "I'll recover."

"Now you'll have to come into my house and take off all your wet clothes, won't you?"

Ned looked at the pensive, muscular man again. He was attractive, with impressive biceps and a chest that had obviously been exercised often.

"I guess I will," Ned said.

They went into the house, which seemed to stretch forever. There were Persian rugs and gold vases and plush white furniture and real murals on the walls—a whole wall full of fauns and nymphs.

The two of them went into the master bedroom, where the director offered Ned a robe made out of blue silk. "I'm not promising to make you a star, is that clear?"

Ned felt a bit chilled by the remark, more than by the water. "It's my own free will," he said.

The director smiled. "Good. I hate to make love to somebody who's crying when I do it."

"I like men."

"Do you like me?"

"Yeah, I like you," Ned said, telling the truth.

The director directed Ned to the waterbed and they lay down side by side, even though Ned was soaked and made a large wet mark on the bedspread.

It turned out that the director did have a part in his new film, at the last moment. It was only ten lines, but Ned studied them as if they were the lead. He stayed in the director's luxurious house while they were making the movie. He and Ned would lie in each other's arms every night and talk about the day's shooting, and the director would ask Ned what he thought might work and what wouldn't, and Ned came up with ideas about everything. Most of the time the director ignored the suggestions, but then Ned noticed the director actually shooting a scene, and then another, the way Ned had suggested.

They rode to the lot together in a limousine at six a.m. every morning and went out to premieres just about every other night. During the day Ned didn't talk to the director very much at all, since the man was besieged by crew members and actors. But at night they talked over dinner and then made love in the huge waterbed, lights from the city shimmering through the bay window in the distance beyond the hills.

Ned wondered what would happen to him when the movie was done. Would the director ask him to leave?

"I'm falling in love with you," the director whispered in Ned's ear that night. "I love your body pressed up next to mine." The man's eyes were intense in the semidarkness.

"You're very . . . nice yourself," Ned said.

"What's going to happen with us later, like next week, when we finish the film?" the director asked, lying down in his boxer shorts on the edge of the bed.

"My agent may have another part for me."

"Do you want to stay with me . . . for a while?"

"The part's in a picture they're shooting in London."

"And you want to leave?"

Ned didn't know what to answer. "Yes and no."

"You want a career, right?"

"Sort of."

"So do I. How about when you get back from London?"

"We could, sure," Ned said.

The director kissed Ned on his lips and his ears and hugged him for almost an hour.

London was a marvelous city, Ned thought, charming as an old dowager gone slightly to seed.

He was the only American in the entire cast and got on well with everyone. Sometimes he thought about the director back in Hollywood, editing the new film. He had several long-distance telephone calls from the man—sad, imploring calls telling Ned how much he missed him, how much he loved him. But Ned of course knew that he'd never see the director again.

But in London he met an Earl, a real Earl who lived on an estate near Pinewood Studios, where the film was being shot. The Earl—Roger by name—would drive over and watch the shooting. He had no job and lived on his income.

He was rather shy and rarely spoke to anyone, but one day Ned and the Earl were in the studio cafeteria line together.

"Any brown sugar for my tea?" the Earl asked the cashier.

"All out."

"There's some honey in that bottle," Ned said, turning to the Earl.

"That should do nicely," the Earl said.

"Are you into health foods?" Ned asked.

"A bit. Yourself?"

"Off and on," Ned replied.

They sat together at one of the tables, and that was the start. The Earl invited Ned to dinner one evening, and Ned accepted. The Earl had a soft, white smile and round, red-speckled cheeks and was trying to make his yellow mustache get bushier. He was interested in opera and sword-collecting, and actually had five servants on the estate.

They dined by candlelight, with two footmen to serve them, and it didn't seem the least bit extravagant. Roger talked about opera and the play he was writing, and Ned ate filet mignon and strawberries and wanted to reach across and touch Roger's hand.

"What's the play about?" he said instead.

"About young men who fight in a war and almost get killed, but manage to survive. It's a play about survival, I suppose," Roger looked up, across the table, as though he'd articulated to himself for the first time what the play was really about.

"And do you think you can get it produced?"

"I have a friend who's very interested in it. And even if that all falls through, I can afford to produce it myself."

"You mean in London?"

"Yes, but I thought a preliminary showing at the Royal Court Theatre might be in order. It's not exactly a commercial play."

"When will it be finished?"

"Any day now. I've worked on it for a year."

"I hope I'll be able to see it."

"You will," Roger smiled. "I want you to be in it."

"In it?"

"I've seen you acting in this current film, and I've talked to you, and I've been impressed."

"Really?"

"Quite sincerely." Roger smiled again. "You've got tons of talent."

"But I'm an American."

"I've noticed. It's a play with an international cast. All sorts of nationalities are in a prison camp together."

"I accept," Ned said.

"Wonderful. You'll be great."

Ned wanted to spend the night, but it turned out that Roger wasn't gay.

"I just think you can act. No sex necessary," he said, and he drove Ned back to his flat near the studio.

The play opened to terrific reviews. Ned was singled out as the outstanding member of a fine cast. Soon after, the play moved to the West End. It was an awesome success there too. "The finest, most moving performance by a young actor I have ever seen," The *Times* critic wrote. "It's a rare phenomenon to find excitement, intellectual integrity, and moral uplift all in one threatrical performance, but last night I found it," said the *Guardian*'s reviewer.

Invitations started pouring in. Ned went out to parties in expensive, breathtaking flats in Mayfair, to outdoor extravaganzas at country homes. People couldn't be nice enough to him. He was flattered and petted, and people laughed at his jokes. Sometimes he would get into serious discussions with intellectuals who made him feel as if he were playing in Chekhov, so intensely did they discuss the play and the way he interpreted his role. He tried to think back to the gray days in Des Moines, but they seemed millions of light-years away. Here, he was surrounded by witty and creative people. Everybody was lovely, and those who weren't lovely were intelligent, ingratiating, or amusing.

In between the performances and the parties, Ned managed to write a play himself, and because of his acting success, he had no trouble getting it produced. It wasn't such a bit hit as the Earl's play, but it was enthusiastically received, and money started to come in. What captured everyone's attention was the hero of the play, who was gay. No apologies, no trauma, no shame. It was as if all the objections of previous centuries had been swept away finally, irrevocably, in this new play, and everyone who attended the theatre wanted to see it. Ned stood in the rear of the theatre during Thursday matinees, when he wasn't acting in the Earl's play, and listened in rapture to the applause filling the theatre. "A play that has done more for liberalizing sexual attitudes than any other work of this century," the reviewer in the *Evening Standard* wrote.

"I'd like to have a child by you," a woman said to Ned at the back of the theatre after the matinee.

"I beg your pardon?"

"Aren't you the author of this play? I've seen you on the stage, Mr. Galveston. I admire you immensely. Forgive me for being so forward, but I really would like to have your child. It's sure to be handsome and gifted."

Ned stared at the woman, who was a beautiful brunette with impassioned eyes—athletic-looking, self-possessed, wearing a white jacket with black buttons.

"I'm afraid I wouldn't make a very good father," Ned said, starting to leave.

"Get to know me better. I promise not to rape you."

They went out for coffee, and surprisingly she was not insane. She conversed intelligently on all subjects and made it quite clear that she'd planned to have Ned's baby only after thinking about it carefully.

"I don't think it would be right," Ned said.

"My husband is sterile. I'd take the child with me when I leave—I'm moving to another continent."

"But why *my* child?" he persisted.

"Don't you want to be immortal?" she asked.

It was a boy, and the mother kept her word and flew away to another part of the world. For some reason that he couldn't explain Ned felt happy, indeed ecstatic, even though he'd probably never see his child again. Somehow knowing that he was alive in another body, his son's body, filled him with joy.

In fact, he wrote a new play about having a child and never seeing it, and this play did even better than the first one. He was signed to play the part in the movie version.

It was the night he won the Oscar that Ned also met Larry, who was an architect, with tender brown eyes and a hard, compact body, somehow a combination of disdain and aggression and playfulness that Ned couldn't resist. Larry didn't know who Ned was since he didn't go to the theatre or to movies very often. All he knew was that Ned and he clicked at the party after the Awards, and they moved in together three weeks after they'd met.

For the first time in his twenty-four years Ned found out what mutual love could be. He and Larry supported each other, and yet they didn't stifle one another. They could talk or not talk, depending on their moods. At any given moment, one seemed to understand the other's needs. Their love-making was spectacular at the beginning but cooled down, of course, after the first year. Still, they would find themselves reunited after a period of quietude, and the love-making flared even higher than it had during those first few months. Ned had felt warmly toward others in the past, like the director, but now he realized what joy there could be in pleasing another person. He wanted to do things for Larry— buy him gifts, leave him little love-notes, compliment him, hold him. And Larry wanted to do the same for Ned. Their two lives blended and interwove and yet they managed to remain their separate selves, each with a career, goals, accomplishments. It lasted fourteen years, and mellowed into a love affair that no other person could ever alter.

But time altered it. Larry died soon after their fifteenth anniversary, and Ned felt shattered. He wept often and couldn't write. He wanted to do nothing and see nobody. He sat in a stupor for days on end, or slept as if he were dead.

But gradually he recovered. He started to mingle in society again, started reading his mail once more and discovered a letter from a group devoted to exposing cruelty and infringement of rights in business and government. Ned flung himself into the work with a diligence he'd never known before. He wrote pamphlets and books, he worked on committees, he made speeches on panels and on television, he met people who ran governments. At first the public resented the group because it made them uncomfortable. But after a while people began to see how much Ned's group was accomplishing. Laws started to change. Corruption and cruelty dwindled. People inflicted less pain on one another. Throughout the whole civilized world a spirit of kindliness and helpfulness began to develop. And Ned was right in the midst of all this activity, and he stayed there for the rest of his life, respected and admired by those who worked with him, feared by the selfish and despotic and exploitative, at ease within his own soul as he'd never been before. How good it is to be alive, he often thought.

The myth is over now.

The myth is over now.

free and easy

I had just come rainbows in the eager mouth of some black guy over in the corner when I spotted him. I wiped my cock with my handkerchief and squeezed the black guy's shoulders. He got up and patted my ass and said thanks.

I walked across the semidarkness and touched the chest of this other guy. I could tell he worked out—a chest that wouldn't stop. Nipples like gumdrops, gumdrops with a little sweat on 'em. I took one in my mouth and bit it gently. He ran his hand over my chest and seemed to like what he felt. We looked at each other up close. He had a brown mustache, I think, and eyes that looked like wild stars. He offered me a hit of amyl and put his hand on my crotch, which was damp because I'd been there over an hour. Then I noticed that someone was doing him in the back, somebody in leather chaps, I think.

—Whatcha up to? he said. And squeezed my cock. A beefy, masculine voice.

—I just came . . . But I wanted to feel your chest.

—Mutual, he said.

We smiled, an inch away from each other's mouths. His breath didn't smell too bad. Great face—like G.I. Joe's. I felt his balls. They were wet, but hung warm and full in my fingers.

I kissed him. Our tongues were dry. I wondered if he could smell the cum on my beard.

—You taste great, he said.

—So do you.

He held my head with both hands and rimmed my ear. It felt like God was doing it.

I licked his Adam's apple. —Hmm, you're *good*, he said.

I looked into his flickering eyes. —Had a successful night on the town? I asked.

—I guess I wouldn't be here if I had, he said, shrugging.

—What time is it?

—After three. He massaged my biceps and leaned down and sucked the hair under my arm.

When we kissed again, I tasted my own salt.

The guy behind him stopped licking and started to move away, still on his knees.

—I was just about to go home, he said.   You're welcome to come.

I stroked his waist. —I don't know if I can get it up.

He stroked my waist. —Sure?

I hesitated for a second. —Maybe. Sure. Okay. I'd like to get together with you.

—Me too.

We hugged and he pulled up his pants and I zipped up. We made our way through the bodies and went into the hallway.

—Where do you live? I said.

—Not far.

—Let me stop in here for a minute. I pointed to the john.

—Sure thing. You're hot.

I went in and took a piss, and took a moment to give my moist cock a final wipe with some toilet paper.

I came back out.

And he had left.

heritage

"Cara, I'd like to see you for a minute!" Ivy called.

Cara lifted the magazine off her sweating face and squinted because of the sun, but didn't move. Several of the other sunbathers looked over at Ivy and whispered to each other.

"Cara! I'd like to *see* you!" *Damn her, she's impossible! I'm going to change my will, I swear it!* Ivy thought. *Bringing packs of women here at all hours of the day and night, no regard for my feelings, none at all! I won't have it! And that damn radio's too loud, and that bowl of potato salad is going to attract flies as sure as I'm sitting here!*

Ivy put her large hands on the arms of the chair, about to rise. "Cara, did you hear me?"

Cara got up and adjusted the straps of her swimsuit and came over to the upper deck. "What is it now, Ivy?"

"Tell those fat-asses they can't *both* sit on that chaise. Don't they have any sense!"

Cara looked at the two women holding hands on the chaise longue. "It's strong."

"When I gave it to you, I didn't mean for it to be wrecked in two days!"

Cara slumped her shoulders. "It's *my* party. I've only had two since I've been here."

"But it's my house!" Ivy threw herself back into the deck chair, almost breaking it.

"Why don't you come and join us?" Cara put her thin, flushed face next to the slats in the railing.

Ivy swept her arm toward the dozen women sunbathing on the far side of the lower deck. "They're all kids!"

"Come on, Ivy. You look very nice today. Is that a new sweater?"

Ivy touched her blue breast and smiled. The sweatshirt had "Pussy Galore" stitched in silver across the front. "You think it's funny?" She tapped the words on her large breasts.

"It's very handsome."

"You're looking very pretty yourself." Ivy thought Cara had gotten too much sun, the face overripe. *I wonder if she really thinks I look good. Or just old-fashioned.* She touched her short hair, then looked back at the women on the lower deck. None of them had hair as short as hers, she noticed. And none of them was dressed butch.

"I'm too old-style to hang around with your crowd," Ivy said. She crossed her legs at the knee, like a man. She felt hot in the sweatshirt and sweatpants.

"You don't look old, so why act it?"

Ivy smiled by puckering her lips. "You want to play chess after they leave?"

"Well . . . I'm supposed to go back into the city for dinner. To Beth's place."

"Oh, I see."

"We can play some other time, all right?"

"You're running around so much I hardly see you . . ."

"Ivy," Cara said gently, looking down at the redwood slats, scratching one eyebrow, "when I moved in here, I didn't promise . . . I didn't promise to be your daughter."

"All I want is some consideration! Is that too much to ask? After all, you'll get my apartments when I die."

"You know I appreciate that. But you're not going to die, Ivy, and you know it!" Cara grinned.

"Got to die sometime." She pushed up the sleeve of her sweatshirt. "See how my skin looks. Like old rubber."

"Your skin looks fine!"

"I looked at myself in the marsh water the other day, and I realized that I'm sixty-three, with only so much time left, and I don't want to spend it with a lot of aggravation. Like all these women coming here and making noise and breaking things and—"

"You've stopped putting that blonde rinse on your hair, haven't you?"

Ivy tugged at some hair near her ear. "Got to face the gray sometime. You don't have to worry of course. You're only twenty-three."

"Twenty-four next month."

"I looked at myself in the marsh water and I saw this ancient dyke staring back at me—with a big, round, fat face."

"Ivy!"

"It's true! I don't have that many years left, so at least give me some peace and quiet, okay! With some good friends like you . . ." She waved the back of her hand at the others. "But not this dyke orgy!"

"You told me I could live here like it was my own place."

"Well, there are limits, Cara."

"We're just having an ordinary party, for god's sake!"

"Your friends get on my nerves."

"And you're rude to them."

"Well, you're rude to me!"

"I am not."

"This is what I get for leaving all my property to you!"

"It was your idea, not mine."

Ivy put her fists on her thighs and bent from the waist. "You want me to take it back?"

Cara shook her head sadly. Her eyes were the color of faded carbon paper. "It's *your* will."

Ivy felt ashamed. "I'm sorry. I don't mean to sound like I'm threatening you." She swatted at a fly but missed.

Cara came up the three steps to the upper deck and sat on the floor near her. "I don't know how to say this exactly, Ivy, but sometimes . . ."

"Yeah?"

"Sometimes you sound like some old . . . old man."

"Thanks. I needed that."

Cara poked at the floor. "Well, you hold that will over me like a weapon."

"We have a contract." Ivy crossed her legs again. She suddenly felt heavy and thirsty and yet didn't want to get up.

"I appreciate what you're doing for me, really I do." Cara reached up and touched Ivy's leg. "But please don't start making me *hope* you die."

Ivy caught her breath; she felt a stab of pain behind her eyes. "Don't you think I feel funny knowing you'll benefit when I croak? I don't want to have to buy your love . . ."

"I don't want to be like some child from another century who had to wait around and smile and kiss ass and fluff up the pillows on her father's death bed."

"That's a shitty thing to say."

"I know . . ."

They both dropped their eyes, and Ivy stuck her fingers into the back of her mouth, to press on the sore spot. "I think I broke a tooth or something," she said.

"Want me to look at it?"

"Oh, it'll be all right."

"Why do you just sit here, Ivy? I thought you liked parties."

"People annoy me nowadays. I'm getting crochety . . . and I can't seem to help it."

Cara looked at a piece of driftwood that Ivy had set on the edge of the flower pot. "Is that new?"

"Found it yesterday." Ivy got up and brought over the piece of driftwood. "Looks like a gingerbread boy, don't you think?"

Cara held the wood and ran her finger over the brown, weathered surface. "Sort of."

"Makes two I found this week. You can probably sell my collection for a pretty penny, one day. Especially since good driftwood seems to be harder and harder to find. You think it's the pollution?"

"Maybe." Cara handed back the gingerbread boy and then stroked Ivy's fingers; she smelled of marsh water.

For a moment Ivy looked at the round wooden head with the chunk missing. "Seems like there aren't as many wild birds in the marsh anymore either . . ."

"Ivy . . . you're making me feel real awkward," Cara said, drawing her legs up under her. "There's something happening between us—"

"Now look at that whore!" Ivy said, standing up. "Now *that's* too much, and that's all there is to it!" She pointed at a girl with oily frizzled hair who'd taken off her blouse and was dancing to a song on the radio. "You can see everything she's got!"

"She's not hurting anybody."

"I don't need her tits hanging out! I don't need it!"

"Ivy, calm down!"

"Get out of here!" Ivy shouted at the girl. "Get out of here!"

"Ivy! You're making more noise and fuss than anybody else!"

"Listen, it's my house and my section of the deck. And if you don't like it, then move!" Ivy's eyes darkened until they were the deep brown of the salt marsh. "What do you say to that, Miss Renter?"

Two women—both blonde, one young and one old, one thin and one heavy—are stacking firewood in the shed Ivy built several years before. Their hands are dirty and Cara has a splinter near the base of her thumb, but they're laughing.

"And then finally this gal swoops off the barstool and kisses me and says she wants me!"

"And you didn't even know her?"

"Never laid eyes on her before."

"What'd you do?"

"Kissed her back—what else!" Ivy wipes some of the dirt on her corduroys. "Turns out her name was Josie and we started living together the very next week."

"So that's how you met Josie!"

"She was a terrific lover. Always thought of me first—and lips on her that just wouldn't stop!" Ivy puts the last two chunks of wood on the stack that is as tall as she is. "Well, that ought to keep us in fuel for a while!"

Cara grabs her from behind as Ivy stoops to leave.

"Hey, what's this?"

Cara hugs her hard from behind. "Just want to show how much I like you."

Ivy pats the small, dirty hands that have come together over her stomach. "Well, I like you too."

"I really should help pay for this firewood. I feel guilty."

"My treat."

"At least let me pay my utility bills!"

"No way!" Ivy says.

"Please!"

Ivy pats Cara's hands again. "Hey, I'm not just your land-lady, I'm your friend."

"Ivy, you're terrific, do you know that?" Cara says, with another squeeze.

She's bringing him here again! Ivy thought, looking out the window. *How could she sleep with somebody like that! He's so dark and hairy. She's only doing it to show how versatile she is. Cock and balls! Cock and balls and hair! Ugh! They're coming over here! Jesus Christ!*

"Ivy! Are you home?" Cara called.

Maybe if I don't answer, they'll go away.

"Ivy?"

"What is it?"

"I'd like you to meet a friend of mine."

Ivy went out and stood on the doorstep. The evening air was damp and cold, her bathrobe not warm enough. And she had a headache.

"Ivy, I'd like you to meet Eduardo."

"Sure," she said, barely looking at him.

"How are you tonight?" He asked her. He was stocky and wide-shouldered, wearing an Army jacket. He had big ears and several days' growth of beard and long, black sideburns.

"You two go to a show?" Ivy asked.

"To the ballet," Eduardo said.

"I see you two around here a lot lately," Ivy said to Cara.

"We've been seeing each other."

"Planning to stay the night again?" She looked right into Eduardo's eyes.

He looked embarrassed.

Cara stared hard at Ivy, her eyes angry. "We haven't decided yet."

Eduardo looked up. "I'm sorry if we've . . ."

"You can be AC-DC if you want to!" she said to Cara.

"Thanks for the permission," Cara smiled.

Eduardo's supposed to be AC-DC too, Ivy thought. *You don't even know where you stand anymore!* "I'd invite you in," she said, "but I didn't clean today."

"I was going to ask if you'd like to have a drink with us," Cara said. "Or smoke some pot."

"Some other time, maybe."

Cara looked at Eduardo. "Do you mind if I talk to Ivy for a minute?"

"Sure," he said, taking out a key. He went over and unlocked Cara's apartment and went inside.

"He's got his own key now?" Ivy said, furious.

"And why not?" Cara looked thin and sinister in the near dark.

"I don't rent to *two* people, that's why."

"He's not living here."

"Looks like he might be considering it."

"Shhh. He might hear you."

"Let him. I'm not afraid of him."

"He's a nice guy, and I don't want you insulting him."

"Are you taking in boarders now?"

"Ivy, you're getting to be like my mother!"

"I'm nobody's mother!"

"The reason I left home was to get away from this same kind of interference."

"You're the one who's interfering! With my property!"

"You're mad if I bring women here. And you're mad if I bring a man!"

"Why can't you make up your mind who you are!"

"I'm being *who* I am—if you don't mind!"

"Well, if you don't like the way I run my property . . ." Ivy massaged her temple, trying to get rid of the headache.

"I pay you rent."

"You haven't paid a single utility bill since you came!"

"You wouldn't let me!"

"Well, nobody's forcing you to stay here!"

"You know I got laid off! It's not right for you to manipulate me like this."

"How can you stand that creep? He's so . . . macho!"

"About as macho as you are, Ivy!" Cara said, holding her voice down.

The headache struck both temples now. "Well, if you're going to marry him, you won't be needing my will to live on, right?"

"You said you *gave* it to me!"

"You weren't sleeping with men then!"

"Yes, I was!"

"Well, I didn't see them!"

"I'll sleep with whoever— Never mind!"

"I'm only trying to keep you from getting a disease. Didn't you say you got a rash from him?"

"I'm willing to risk it. Thanks for your concern."

"I'm not trying to boss you around."

"But you *are*, Ivy! Don't you even see it?"

Ivy stuffed her hands into the pockets of the bathrobe. "Don't you think you owe me something? You don't spend nearly as much time with me as you used to."

Cara adjusted the collar of her knitted sweater against the cold air. "Maybe I should . . . but you seem to pick at me all the time."

"I'm sorry. And I know better than to demand that you spend time with me. I have no right to do that . . ."

"Does that mean you're going to stop?"

"All those women were bad enough! But a *man*! I feel like you've betrayed me!"

"I need both men and women. Maybe you need to—"

"Listen, I don't need anything. I lived with Josie for eight years, till she became such a pain in the butt I couldn't stand her! I'm too old. Who needs all these complications! Who needs 'em!"

Cara moved, and the deck boards squeaked. "Let me live my life, please! Is that a lot to ask?"

"You promised you'd stay with me! That's why I gave you my will! You promised me!"

"Are you going to disinherit me?" Cara said spitefully.

Ivy pulled her bathrobe around her chest. "You make me want to!"

"I'm going to hurt your feelings, I suppose, but I've got to speak my mind anyway." Cara stared defiantly at her.

"Well?"

Cara backed down. "Listen, I've never even seen that will. It's still in the sealed envelope you gave me. So I don't even know what it says, and—"

"It says I leave you *everything*. All my money and both my apartments. And I have some stocks, too. I never mentioned those before." She stopped, "Cara, I feel real stupid trying to bribe you like this."

"Then stop trying to own me!"

Ivy stepped back and shivered. She could see Eduardo watching them from the kitchen. She couldn't speak, her feelings in a jumble. Her whole body felt cold. Why was Cara doing this to her! She'd promised her everything! Everything! All those years, those tedious hours she'd worked in crummy jobs, saving her money, investing. She'd left it all to Cara, and now Cara didn't want to pay attention to her! She looked at the other houses on the boardwalk, silhouetted in the half moon. They stood on slim stilts in the salt marsh.

She pushed her cold hands deeper into the pockets of the bathrobe. "You don't get anything for free in this world," she said.

"Why would I *want* to be with you, Ivy? You've become such an old meddling busybody. An old grouchy grandpa!"

"Damn it, I *will* disinherit you! Don't push me too far!"

Cara's face looked pained. "I need the money, damn it! I've already earned it!"

"I've helped you, and I've asked for almost nothing in return."

"Ivy, do you know what you are? A leftover. I'm sorry, but you *are!* A dried-up old dyke in silly sweatshirts! You're sort of pathetic, do you know that?"

Two women are sitting in front of the warm fireplace in Ivy's front room. They are both dressed in sloppy shirts with rips under the arms. On their laps are some cracker crumbs. The chess board is still out, but abandoned.

"Have you read the new Audubon *yet?" Cara asks.*

Ivy picks it up from the coffee table. "Not yet. You want it back?"

"Keep it till you're finished. There's supposed to be an interesting article about eagles."

"Yeah, I want to read that."

"Want to read it together?"

"Love to," Ivy sits on the sofa next to Cara and opens the magazine.

"Isn't that gorgeous!" Cara says, pointing to a picture of two eagles circling above a golden hillside.

"Wonder if they're going to be able to save 'em," Ivy says, shaking her head. "Look here. They've listed the dangers."

She points at the page.

"*Who could kill things so majestic!*" *Cara says.*

"*Some people just have no feelings, I guess. I'm going to write a letter to somebody.*"

"*Let's both write one. That's the only way anything gets done.*"

"*Want to do it now?*" *Ivy asks.*

"*Let's see what the article mentions first, okay?*"

"*I moved over here because of the wild birds and the fresh air and the clear water. People ought to have all that in their lives, don't you think? That's not too much to ask, is it?*" *Ivy cocks her head.*

"*Absolutely.*"

Ivy says, "We have so much in common, God, I love talking to you!"

There was a rap on the door. *She's probably come to apologize*, Ivy thought.

She opened the door. "Yes?"

"Do you have a minute?"

"Is he gone?"

"He left this morning."

"I didn't see him go."

"I'm sorry about what I said last night."

"That's all right. Want a mug of coffee? Just made some." She went to the stove and picked up the pot.

Cara sat down at the dining table. She riffled through the Sunday comics that Ivy had been reading.

"You think we might go for a ride today, Cara? We can use my car."

Cara looked up. She didn't look rested.

"I didn't mean what I said. I'm not going to take back my will. I'm sorry I flew off the handle like that. I don't know what comes over me any more." She poured two mugs of coffee and sat down opposite Cara. "I didn't mean a word of what I said. You're everything I have, just about. All my friends have turned on me. Never did care much for my family, and most of them are dead anyhow. I sure don't want to start drinking again, and I can't spend all my time watching the egrets in the marsh, can I?"

Cara gave a tiny smile and took a sip of her coffee.

"If you don't feel like talking, that's all right. Feels good just to have you sit here and listen. You chat if you want to, but I don't mind if you don't feel like it. You know me—I never get tongue-tied. Nothing worse than a tongue-tied lesbian!" She smiled, then buttered a piece of bread and cut it in two. "Want some bread and butter?"

Cara shook her head no.

"I just love bread and butter dipped in coffee. With the Sunday paper." She took a bite. "I'm real glad you came over, Cara. I want you to know that. Basically you're a very nice person."

Cara wasn't looking at her. "I've—I've brought you something." She reached into the back pocket of her jeans and pulled out a folded manila envelope. "Not a present, I'm afraid." Her voice was tight.

"What's that?" She already knew and fought the sick feeling in her stomach.

"It's your will."

"What about it?"

"I've decided it's best to give it back to you. I'm sorry."

"But you need it." Ivy felt a raw spot open in her heart.

"I've decided to move."

She looked down at the wrinkled envelope. "You're not going to marry Eduardo, are you?"

"No, I'm going to get an apartment in the city."

"But why?"

"Because I want to."

"But what about our friendship?"

Cara toyed with the salt shaker, the words coming out very small. "I want to be myself . . ."

Ivy dipped the bread and butter into the coffee. "But . . ." She felt numb. "I won't bug you any more. I promise."

Cara tapped the salt shaker on the table. "Yes, you will. You can't help it."

"No, I promise." She reached over.

But Cara moved her hands. "Don't, please. It's . . . hard enough."

"But, Cara, please!" Ivy slapped at the tears in her eyes. She dipped some more bread into the mug and took a bite.

It tasted like garbage. "Please, Cara!" she said with her mouth full.

"Don't beg, Ivy!"

"Please, Cara! Don't go!" She got up and put her arms around Cara's slender body. "Please. You're all I have!"

Cara broke the hug gently and got up. "Goodbye, Ivy. Let's make it as brief as possible. I'm sorry."

She left the will on the table, and Ivy stared at it until the bread and butter turned into ugly, brown mush in her mouth.

how will we recognize evil when we see it, and what will we do about it if we do?

The Chancellor's strong teeth—all of them his own at age seventy, however wired by helpful dentists through the years—bit down on his words: "Let's fire the cocksucker!" His tuft of plastic-stiff white hair shook on his head like the comb of a turkey-cock. "Who the hell does this asshole think he is?" The Chancellor's wattles turned hot with rage, and he flung the sheet of paper he was holding onto the xerox machine in the Dean's office. "I want to see his head on a plate by tomorrow noon," he said. He stood tall, a large, slightly stooped man, as energetic as he had been at forty. Maybe his paunch was bigger, soggier, but he kept his suit coat buttoned so that it wouldn't show. He wasn't about to become one of those old men he'd read about—actually getting smaller; he was taller, healthier than he'd ever been in his life, ten times more robust than he'd been as that puny, asthmatic Idaho boy he had despised. Yes, a lot of man in a pale-blue seersucker suit, with sturdy, well-nourished bones like metal rods.

"I'm not sure we can fire him," the Dean replied, made-up with a cosmetic smile and blinking at the same time. "We could have some trouble." The Dean was a "cocksucker" himself, among other things, as well as the dean of the extension university that offered courses on military bases in Asia, and so he was nervous about that particular term of abuse. "Perhaps we all ought to reprimand the boy." The Dean spoke in a flouncy Southern voice dripping with oil. To the casual eye he seemed inoffensive and vague. But he was supercilious and unctuous with inferiors, cowardly with superiors, and knowledge of his approaching death from Hodgkin's disease only made him less brave, not more. He lived in constant terror that someone in the military one night would discover him sucking Japanese penises in a shadowy park and his career would be over. Believing that the military would never change its attitude toward homosexuality, he endured the autocracy and insults of the Chancellor, always smiling his fruity Southern-Belle smile, believing that nobody imagined he was "gay," although of course everybody from the Chancellor down to the secretaries knew it the first time he opened his mouth.

"Write this down!" The Chancellor waited until the Dean got a pen and note pad. "Send out a notice to all the faculty, both full-time and part-time, telling them it is *not* their business to run down this university—they're getting paid to teach! We're not paying them to make fun of what I, single-handedly, have set up and kept going for the past twenty-four years!" The Chancellor's aggrieved eyes grew nostalgic with memory.

"Yes, I was thinking of that myself," the Dean agreed, wiping the sweetish moisture from his upper lip.

The Chancellor looked at the Assistant Dean, who was standing by a filing cabinet. The man resembled a porcupine—or maybe Mighty Mouse, with enormous ears protruding from his stringy brown hair. "And tell them that if they don't like teaching over here, they can get the hell back to the States—and see if they can find a job over there!" He bared all his teeth again; only this time it was a smile. Or at least the Dean and Assistant Dean thought it was a smile, and so they smiled too.

The Chancellor picked up the paper he had flung onto the xerox machine and read it again. It was a "report" that Sam Lowell, the education director in Okinawa, had sent to the Dean about a political science instructor, because the instructor had appeared on a closed-circuit TV show. Instead of plugging the courses, he had said such things as, "It's really only a fourth-rate junior college, though it presumes to give college credits that transfer" and "The only requirements to take a course are $84 and a pencil—and if you don't have the pencil, that's okay." The education director, who prided himself on having the largest enrollment of all the centers, had not been pleased, not at all.

"Maybe he didn't say those things," the Assistant Dean suggested. "Perhaps he was misunderstood. I know Gil, and he wouldn't do this to us. He was so grateful to find a job last year." The Assistant Dean had begun to twitch, an unfortunate tic that often invaded his entire body. Very unbecoming in Mighty Mouse, or the "twitchy porcupine," as the faculty called him. He was a short man, "brave" only when he was drunk, which was often, faint-voiced the rest of the time. It seemed impossible to believe that he had been a speech teacher before becoming Assistant Dean, for he had a scared, phlegmy voice whenever he spoke to anyone, either publicly or privately. Since he was a homosexual, like the Dean, he was blinking hard today too. The Chancellor's semiannual visit was never pleasant, but this time it was triply upsetting because of the "report" on Gil Luscier's downgrading the university.

"If you ask me, he sounds like a fag!" the Chancellor spat. He stared at the two men in front of him in the Dean's handsome office. "Who else but a fag would say such 'witty' things!"

"I don't think that would be a good line to pursue—" the Dean began.

"Who the hell says it wouldn't?" The Chancellor interrupted. "If he's a queer, by god we'll ride him out of this program on a rail! How do they get through our security clearance in the first place?" He glared at them with contempt. "Just who do these queers think they are these days! Did you know that back on campus the local queer club actually hired themselves a lawyer and made the university give them eighteen hundred dollars because it's a bona-fide campus organization!" He shook his head in bewilderment.

The Japanese mail-boy popped his head into the office to see if there was any mail to be picked up, but the Dean shooed him away. "Bona-fide, my ass!" the Chancellor concluded.

"No one has ever accused Gil of that particular . . . offense," the Assistant Dean gulped, wishing he had a drink, several drinks.

"Is he married?" the Chancellor asked, knowing that neither of the deans was.

"No, he's not married," the porcupine admitted.

"How old is he?"

"About thirty."

The Chancellor rubbed his calloused palms together, making a rasping noise. "Thirty years old and not married, eh? Well, that sounds pretty queer to me! And I thought you two'd keep up on such things!" the Chancellor said, waving the "report" at them.

After looking at the Assistant Dean, the Dean said, "Gil's grades were pretty low last term . . ."

"Can we screw him on that? But maybe he likes being screwed, if he's a queer and all. I *told* you it was a good idea to make the faculty turn in their grade percentages." He took the record from the Dean's hand and scrutinized it. "So he gave four F's and five D's in one course, eh? Obviously the man's an incompetent. Because he can't improve the students, he tries to degrade the whole system! Somebody ought to spank his butt in public!"

"Generally there have been good reports on his teaching," the Dean had to admit.

"I don't give a good rusty about his teaching! All our teachers are good teachers, damn good teachers! We can get good teachers by the cartload if we want them. What we don't need are any fairy malcontents who shoot off their mouths — and over TV yet!" The Chancellor looked meditative for a second. Then his wide, pushed-in face sprouted a grin. "You two ever heard that he fools around with his male students?"

Mighty Mouse began to get short of air, feeling his voice get breathier. Still he couldn't control the sound, despite all those years of speech classes. "I haven't heard that about him . . . no, no."

"Nor me," the Dean said.

"Well, I'll bet somebody has heard about this cocksucker!" The Chancellor kicked the Dean's overstuffed black chair in fury, leaving a dusty mark. "We'll get something on the son of a bitch, you watch me if I don't."

The Assistant Dean glanced over at the Dean surreptitiously. His necktie was choking him despite the air conditioning. He could feel the threatening Asian air lurking outside the windows, just waiting to invade the room.

Suddenly the Chancellor erupted again, making ugly furrows in his forehead. He wagged the paper back and forth. "It's a good thing Luscier made these notes for his smart-ass talk and Sam got ahold of 'em. We've got him good!"

The Assistant Dean wanted to help. "I noticed that he wrote 'If I was you' on the page. He may have said that over the air."

"Yeah?" the Chancellor said. "So what?"

The Mouse tried to clear the phlegm from his throat, without success. "Well, I thought we could say he used the wrong *mood*—instead of the subjunctive, when he's supposed to be teaching the students to be educated."

The Chancellor wanted to dismiss this big-eared twerp with a flip of his hand. But he never let anything go to waste, even this "turd argument," as he called it to himself. Perhaps he could use it against the Assistant Dean if he ever needed to get rid of him.

He sniffed, then looked down, and read from the teacher's notes: " 'A person has to drive with his car windows rolled up on US bases in Asia or somebody will shove a bachelor's degree from this university through the window!' Now, I suppose that shitass thinks that's clever. I'll clever him!" He kicked the overstuffed chair again. "Has he ever been reported for wearing long hair in the BX or T-shirts or any other violations like that? We'll send him packing like we did that hippie freak last year!" The Chancellor was enthusiastic with plans, runnels of his heart's blood speeding through the network of arteries and veins, making his pale skin hum with inspiration.

"Well, I think he was seen with the fifteen-year-old son of a colonel, in somewhat compromised circumstances," the Assistant Dean offered, abandoning Gil Luscier, moving in with the other two for the kill.

The Chancellor hardly noticed the fifteen-year-old Thai girl who was popping ping-pong balls out of her vagina, so involved was he in telling Art Lovelace about what had happened to the political science instructor who had criticized the university. "Boy, did that piglet squawk! Turns out he was a frigging pansy after all. And I fired that sissy sneak so fast his head spun. In person! Those two old aunties who call themselves our Dean and Assistant Dean didn't have the balls to do it. I don't know why the fuck I keep them around." He snorted. He liked Art Lovelace. He and Art had gone to plenty of whorehouses in Bangkok together. Art was an all-right guy. "All I did was give him half his salary for the rest of this year and told him to grab his bags and git."

"Get a load of the chick with the filter-tip cunt," Art said, pointing to the girl on the small, raised stage who was smoking a cigarette with her vaginal lips.

"Now I call that evilosity!" the Chancellor smirked, using one of his favorite words.

"You ought to see her with a pipe," Art joked, leaning back in his chair in the surprisingly cheerful night club. He seldom referred to academic matters, like the firing of the teacher, because he was a politician, a wheeler-dealer, a puffy-faced playboy whose preoccupations were beer and pornography. He was one of the extension university's administrators, in charge of the Thailand division. When the Chancellor came over for his semiannual "fuckfest," as Art termed it, he worked hard to make the old man feel horny and to round up some far-out lays. The rest of the time Art went to live sex shows, ate in fine restaurants, and drank lots of beer.

The Chancellor licked his ample lips when the girl rose from her stool and stuck the cigarette toward his face. "Hey, I'll burn my mouth!" he said, but he stood up and moved closer to the small stage, reached up and touched the girl's slim thigh. She retreated coyly, then returned. The Chancellor stroked her black pubic hair and licked his lips again. The Thai girl stuck out her slithery, long tongue at him and flicked it. The Chancellor got an erection, and gave the girl's pubic hair a tug that made her wince. She dropped the cigarette out of her vagina and backed away, and the Chancellor laughed. Then he kissed his lips at her and looked over his shoulder at Art Lovelace, who gave him a V for victory sign. "Do you think she likes me?" the Chancellor whispered.

"She prefers experienced men," Art said, blowing a smoke ring.

"But I'd break her in two," the Chancellor said, referring to the size of his penis. He beckoned to the girl, who was more experienced than either of the men. "Come here, cutey. I won't pull your pussy anymore. I promise."

Reluctantly the girl moved one step nearer to the edge of the stage, small-boned, totally nude except for high heels. She looked past the Chancellor toward Art for confirmation. What the Chancellor didn't know was that Art had paid the girl fifteen dollars earlier in the day so that she would pay special attention to the man with the white hair. In fact, he always made it a point when the Chancellor visited to give girls an extra fifteen to make a play for the old man.

"Not too many men my age can still get it for free!" the Chancellor snickered.

Art nodded, digesting his beer. What was fifteen bucks or so every six months! You sure couldn't beat Thailand.

"Boy, I'd like to eat her out good," the Chancellor said to Art, but he noted the other patrons, mostly men, Oriental men, through the listless eddies of smoke. Would they know who he was?

"Go ahead. Do it!" Art encouraged him.

The girl came closer still and started to retrieve her fallen cigarette. On impulse the Chancellor jumped up onto the stage and knelt in front of her; she didn't resist. Instead she spread her legs and placed her delicate hands on the nape of his neck and began to massage. The Chancellor buried his mouth in her flesh, tasting the cigarette smoke that lingered, twisting his tongue into the soft folds. The girl began to moan and bump her pelvis against his nose. The Chancellor felt one of his knees crack and then pop, but he forgot the discomfort in his feast.

Suddenly the girl screamed and banged her fists on his stiff white hair, but the Chancellor wouldn't let go. Indeed he gave her soft folds one final bite before he pushed her away and stood up, his knee snapping back into place.

The girl didn't cry, but took off one of her high heels and

held it like a weapon. "You son beach!" she screamed at him.

He held his hands over his head, pretending to be contrite. "Excuse me, baby! Excuse me, my teeth slipped, that's all! I got carried away by your pretty charms!" He started to cough he was laughing so hard, and the girl hobbled backwards a few steps, almost fell, and the Chancellor and Art laughed even harder. After a few seconds, the girl herself laughed and called him something in Thai.

To himself Art was thinking, "I work for an all-American Nazi asshole." But he didn't stop laughing, because the Chancellor liked people around him to laugh, people with a sense of humor.

The Chancellor hesitated about jumping off the stage, and for an instant Art thought of getting up to help, but he realized that that would be a strategic mistake. The Chancellor would take it as a sign that Art considered him old. Better to let him get down by himself, even if he breaks his neck. Some night, on one of these "fuckfests," the old asshole would have a heart attack in the tropical arms of one of these whores and there'd be a bit of explaining to do—to the officials back in the States, to the Chancellor's wife, although Art wasn't too worried about what he'd say when the time came. The military understood what the function of whores was. Maybe the Chancellor's wife did too.

"Jesus, that was fun!" the Chancellor chuckled, still coughing a little, collapsing into the chair. The Oriental men in the smoky room glanced at him without interest, then went back to their private conversations. A tall girl with her pubic hair shaved off, carrying a snake, was coming out onto the stage.

"How did she taste?"

"And my doctor told me to give up smoking too!"

"I think you almost had her coming," Art said.

"A little too young for me. I like 'em about twenty," the Chancellor said in all seriousness.

"Guess what. I got a new batch of hot films. You want to pick up two or three girls from here and head back to my apartment and watch 'em?"

"Let me catch my breath first." The Chancellor lifted his

shirt with two fingers, to allow his sweat to dry. He squirmed in his seat. "And I think my hemorrhoids are starting to act up again."

"That's too bad," Art commiserated. He knew that the Chancellor suffered quite a bit because of his piles. If only the old geek wouldn't talk about them all the time! Yes, he was a geek—that was the word. He should have been on display in a freak show biting the heads off chickens.

"I was telling Colonel Curly Nowak that the Air Force hospitals aren't what they used to be—if they can't cure my hemorrhoids after three different tries!"

"I know something that will make you forget your troubles," Art said.

The Chancellor looked interested. Good old Art could always be counted on to come up with something special! He made all the damn flying around, visiting all the education centers, having to sit in a special strap seat to ease his piles, almost worthwhile. "What's that? Find that two-headed girl who likes to smoke dick that I asked you for?" His eyes twinkled.

"Afraid not. But I've been keeping that special Russian vodka and sturgeon I told you about."

The Chancellor's jaws moved as if he were eating. "You did?"

"Been keeping the both of them in my freezer for the past four months, just for you."

"Oh, Art . . ." The Chancellor was touched. "How nice of you."

"I know how much you liked the last batch I got."

The Chancellor grew almost misty-eyed, grinning his wired-tooth smile. "Sure makes a person feel appreciated when he knows that people will go out of their way . . ." He broke off, tingling with emotion. "You're like family, Art."

"I do it because I like to," Art said, looking straight into his boss's eyes. There wasn't a speck of guile showing anywhere.

"By God, it's nice to know you can count on your friends. It's people like you, Art, who have helped make this the largest college program on military bases in the whole world!"

Art nodded. He had heard the Chancellor give his sales pitch endless times over the years, both with others present and when they were alone. He always stressed the size, not the quality, of the program. *I guess somewhere in that geek's brain of yours there must have been some interest in genuine education some time or other. You say you even have a Ph.D. in psychology. Of course, when you got your degree, they were still offering majors in phrenology!* He looked at the caved-in, peasant face, the broad, nostril-dominated nose of the Chancellor. *Is he a pathetic man? Is he somebody I should feel sorry for? Then why does he seem like such an unadulterated shit?*

The Chancellor took a swallow of his mai tai, his fifth. "I brought college classes to Vietnam!" he said solemnly, addressing himself. "That was the first war—the very first ever—where they had college courses going on right during the conflict! At Cam Ranh Bay and Da Nang. And I did it! I talked General Britter into the whole idea. But you don't get any thanks for it. All you get is a lot of bellyachers and malcontents! We had classes going day and night in Vietnam—before the war stopped." He stared moodily down into his mai tai. "They ought never to forget that."

Art spied the symptoms. The Chancellor was about to cry. Art had been through this evening before, tears and recriminations about how the Chancellor wasn't appreciated, how people forgot what he had done over the years. Not up to a repetition, Art patted the Chancellor's arm affectionately. "Come on, come on, let's get you a girl, and we'll go back to my place and watch my new movies, okay? There's one with a dog this time."

The Chancellor eyed the group of thirty, the new full-time faculty at the sendoff dinner at Travis Air Base that he sponsored every year. "We're not looking for people with radical notions, with weirdo notions about life or sex or education, and I'm telling you straight out tonight that we aren't! We had enough trouble last year with some sex nut, so if you want to keep your jobs, then keep your noses clean!" He let his eyes glide over each one in the group so that all would know he meant business.

"Thank God, I don't see any freaks in this year's group! That's a good start!" the Chancellor added, to show them that he was basically a good-natured guy.

A few faculty heads turned toward each other, but nobody said anything.

"I just wish I was flying over with you tonight," he went on. "But I'll be over in a few months to check up on you!" He laughed and took a sip of water from his glass on the banquet table. He suddenly felt a thud in his chest, and he clutched his ribs with both hands. He went down into the remainder of his strawberry mousse, and then fell on the floor. He groaned a few times and tried to make his heart stop exploding. But he was unsuccessful.

He was sorely missed by the world.

life

"Hi, my name is Francis and I'm an alcoholic."

"Hi, Francis!" the group answered supportively, immediately.

"This is the first time I've ever talked about my life like this, and Sue tells me my time is limited 'cause there's another meeting right after this one, so I'd better hurry if I'm gonna get out my whole story in half an hour, right? I could go on for a couple of years if I'm not careful! And someday I'm gonna write a book about it!" Francis was sitting at the head of the large scarred table, his gray hair straggly and fluffy, like dandelion fuzz; his thick face pug-nosed, soft in the wrong places, especially under the eyes, the loose skin falling away from the nose as if ineptly suspended on a peg. His vest and pants were clean, but wrinkled, the clothes of an old wino, even if the eyes and smile belonged to a reformed man, pale, blue eyes that held past pain like two tiny reservoirs.

"Where should I begin?" Francis said to himself, looking up at the big round clock on the shabby wall opposite him. A couple of latecomers came in and took chairs against the side wall. They lighted cigarettes at once. Already the room was full of gray smoke. Of the thirty people there, at least twenty-five were smoking.

"Well, I suppose I'd better start at the beginning. You see, when I was a little kid I used to follow the ice truck, and so I started going into the local bar with the iceman, and they'd always give me a ginger ale or a coke or something, and so I got used to going to bars."

Several people nodded, and Francis felt encouraged.

"Then the next thing I knew I was a teenager, and that's when I discovered I had a little bit of a homosexual problem." Francis looked up partway to see how shocked his audience was. A chair squeaked as somebody got up for coffee from the table at the rear, but nobody gave any audible reaction. "Not that I regret all the good times I had with guys. You might say I had the best of both worlds, 'cause I liked girls too, and of course I'm married now."

He looked up at the big round clock again, straining to read the numbers, spreading his worn, blunt hands out before him, near Sue's coffee cup. "But I really started drinking, I guess, when I was going to the gay bars—I drank to get my courage up, and pretty soon I was drinking with more courage than anybody else around!" Francis laughed, and so did the group.

"Then later I got married. My wife had three kids from her first marriage, and we got along pretty good. I was working as a laborer, and doing all right. Didn't drink till I got home from the job. You see, I thought I was on top of everything."

Several people in the group nodded their heads in agreement.

"Then finally I started coming home from work and just sitting in this little place I'd made for myself, in the basement among these crates and cardboard boxes. Didn't want nobody to bother me—not my wife, not her kids, not even my *own* kid, Kevin, which we'd had by this time. 'Cause all I wanted was to be left alone with my booze."

An ageing woman with a long body got up for coffee, and Sue, the Coordinator, borrowed a cigarette from the heavy man next to her. Sue had let her teeth become discolored.

"Well, about this time I started driving a cab, and I was really having a time. You see, once I picked up this real pretty blonde-headed girl—she was going to the airport on a vacation. Well, we got to shooting the breeze in the cab, and when we got to the airport she invited me in for a drink. And I joined her and left my cab double-parked outside. Well, here we was, shooting the breeze and having a fine old time, and we finally go outside and there's a big cop looking at my

117

cab. So this girl, Virginia, says she'll take care of it, and she goes over and tells the cop the taxi driver is *inside* the terminal. Well, he goes in to find me, and I sneak out, and me and this Virginia drive over to another parking lot, and the girl says to me, 'Why don't you come to Havana with me?' And I was feeling pretty terrific, you see, and I says, 'Why the hell *not*?' So off we fly to Havana, and I don't remember nothing else except getting on that damn plane!"

Francis looked up at the clock at the rear of the room as he rubbed the lines on his forehead. "Well, so I go along driving my cab once I get back from Havana, and then I lose my license for drunk driving, and so I start working on construction again. That's when things started to get really bad."

A zombie-faced man spilled some coffee at the far end of the table, and when it was cleaned up, Francis went on. "Anyhow, I started not washing myself, and my wife tells me I started to stink to high heaven. Sometimes I even went for three or more weeks without taking a bath and changing my clothes, and to be honest I didn't give a damn. Not one damn. My wife would plead with me and cry, and my kids would cry, and I'd promise to stop, but there I'd be right back where I'd been the day before, down in my little den in the basement, slopping up the booze and stinking like a garbage dump."

Francis looked at the clock.

"Well, I'd better hurry or it's going to take me a week to tell it all!" He laughed. And the others laughed too.

"So I left my wife about this time and started travelling with a carnival. And mostly I ran the ferris wheel, but I did some entertaining too. I remember this one time I was in drag for some reason or other, and I was taking a leak upside the ferris wheel when this big-bellied cop spotted me. You should've seen the look he gave me! Didn't know what to make of me—here was this woman taking a leak outside the ferris wheel! Well, anyway, he pulls me in, and I don't remember what happened exactly after that, except that I finally went back home to my wife and kids."

The smoke in the room was as thick as broth now.

"So I went on drinking and they started carrying me

home from the construction sites. People had to cover for me, and I wasn't worth a damn to nobody. But what finally really did it was breaking my leg 'cause I fell off a building—smashed my ankle all to hell! And there I was trussed up in bed at home. Well, my wife, she'd put the liquor away in the kitchen cabinet so I couldn't get it, you see. But one day when she was out shopping, I pulled myself out of that bed and dragged my body all the way downstairs. The pain was something terrible, and I could've wrecked that pin the doctor had put in my ankle and never walked right again! But all I knew was that I needed a drink! And so I gets up on a kitchen chair and takes a swig. Then I puts the bottle back and climbs off that chair and goes all the way back up to my bed. And then I realize I want another drink. So I climbs all the way *back down* those stairs and up on that kitchen chair and then takes that bottle back to my room!"

A few people in the group coughed because of the cigarette smoke, and several chairs squeaked on the warped floorboards.

"God, I could go on for hours," Francis said, looking at the people around him. "But Sue told me I had only half an hour."

Sue grinned at Francis, showing her decayed teeth.

"So the upshot is, I guess, that I've been on the wagon now for fifteen weeks, and I want to stay on it."

"Right, Francis! You will, Francis! You're doing fine, Francis!" the group said.

"You've got to take it one day at a time, that's what I've learned. Just one day at a time." Francis looked over at Sue. "Is my time up, huh?"

Sue looked at the big round clock on the wall. "You still have some time left."

Francis grinned and rubbed at his puffy eye. "Well, that's the story of my life. I'm fifty-seven years old now, and I've had one hell of a life." He looked up at the big round clock. He still had fifteen minutes left. "You know, I thought it would take longer to tell," Francis said, almost smiling.

beer and rhubarb pie

Something seemed to be bothering him the day he came to repair the back steps of my house. He didn't say anything, but I sensed it in his eyes and in the way he hunched his shoulders. Since I was just his employer I didn't ask him, thinking he'd consider it none of my business. I simply led him up the stairs to the second floor and showed him the two steps that were pulling away from the others. "Think you can fix those?" I asked.

"No sweat," Fernando said, hardly bending over to look.

"I tried fixing 'em myself, but I guess I didn't drive in the nails right, or something."

"I can fix it," he said, taking the hammer out of the holder around his waist. I detected a trace of a Spanish accent.

As he worked, we talked and I found out he was a Cuban exile who'd managed to escape when he was seventeen. He said he'd been beaten up because he'd had some holy cards when the troops rounded up the students at his school. First he'd gone to Miami and then came here to San Francisco. Somewhere along the way he'd been in the Army for two or three years and learned to be a carpenter. He said he still considered himself a Catholic, but that he didn't go to Church anymore. He was thirty-seven, but looked about forty.

He didn't look up at me as he worked on the steps, but I sensed a tension between us. He was wearing an old T-shirt and soiled work pants, with his hair very short and as black as factory smoke. I watched his heavy neck muscles move as he twisted his head from time to time. All in all I found him quite handsome, dark the way I prefer.

"You gay?" he asked abruptly, looking over his shoulder. For some reason I hesitated answering, although I usually wouldn't think twice about it. Maybe it was the intensity in the man's glossy brown eyes or the hammer in his fist. "You doing a survey?" I said.

"I work for lots of gays, that's all," he answered, removing the nails I'd tried to drive in.

I wondered if I looked too typical, with my Levi's and well-exercised body. I'm pale blond too, and to some people that might seem effeminate, just on general principles.

"You're *not* gay, I take it?" I asked him.

"Who me?" He laughed. The lips were a bit chapped and his teeth a little off-color, but somehow everything went well with his dark skin. He had deep squint lines around his eyes. You could tell he would never wear sun glasses, no matter what. I wondered if he was also the kind who'd let guys suck him off without so much as a thank you.

"You married?" I asked.

"Sure. Nice girl. She's from Guatemala."

"Any kids?"

"Yeah. Three." He grabbed the banister and shook it, to see how unsteady the stairwell was. "Good thing you called me. This coulda broke and somebody coulda sued you for everything you got." He grinned at me.

"I'm afraid they wouldn't get much."

"You own this place?"

"I'm making payments, shall we say."

"I'm thinking about buying. We're just renting now."

"Well, you should be able to save on repairs," I said, nodding at his hammer.

"Yeah, I'm really handy around the house. You're not?"

"I get by," I said. "I'm too busy at the moment."

"What do you do for a living?"

I sat several steps below him and noticed the nice ass. "I distribute soft drinks."

"Yeah." He slapped his palm with the hammer head. The hands were scratched and scarred. "I've always worked physical. Feels good." He stood above me and I looked at his crotch, but not for long. That seemed nice too; the flap was crooked near the bottom and the brass zipper showed.

"Where *were* you in the Army?" I asked him.

"Germany mostly. *You* been in the Army?"

"Almost, but the draft ended just in time."

"I had a real good time in Germany—not from the Germans, though. They considered me a nigger. But I fucked a lot."

"Did you?"

"Some nice ass there."

"Well, I'm glad, for your sake."

"You gotta beer by any chance? Man, I'm working up a thirst!"

"Let me check the refrigerator." I went into the house and found a beer on the back shelf behind a box of crackers. When I came back, he'd removed his T-shirt and I could see what a narrow waist he had; his ribs looked like a hungry dog's he was so slim. "This okay?"

He held up the bottle of Miller's. "A beer's a beer!" he said. "Thanks."

"When you've got a real thirst," I said.

"You live here alone?" He took a short swallow and kept his eyes on me as he tilted the bottle.

"I have a friend I share with . . ."

"A guy?"

"Yes . . . He's working today."

"What's he do?"

"He's an accountant."

"Yeah?" A smirk appeared on his face, but he stuck the bottle into his mouth to cover it. "Ahhh! That's great! Join me?"

"I'm afraid that's the last one."

"Take a swig of mine then!" He held out the beer. "I don't have any germs." He laughed.

"I just had some coffee before you arrived, so I'm not thirsty."

He set the bottle on the step above him. "I'm gonna have to cut you some new steps, okay?"

"You'll have to buy some wood then, right?"

"Got some out in the truck that might do."

"That sounds fine," I said.

We stared at each other until I looked down. At the bottom of the staircase I could see the wheelbarrow and the bags of cement and the pile of bricks I'd bought but never used for the new patio.

"So you share with this guy, huh?" he said.

I had Fernando come back a few days later because I wanted some cabinets made for the kitchen. It was sunless and almost cold and he was wearing a suede vest over a winter shirt. "I got it on sale," he said when I complimented him on the vest. "You like it, huh?" He fingered the bottom.

"Very nice." I had a similar one but didn't say so.

"You don't think it makes me look like a faggot, do you?"

"What does a faggot look like?" I replied.

"Oh, you know." He twirled his hand in the air several times.

"Are you afraid of looking like a faggot?"

"I'm not afraid of nothing!" he said sharply.

"Good," I said. I pointed at the space over the sink. "I'd like you to take out these old cabinets and put in two larger ones. And could you paint 'em cornbread yellow?"

"Cornbread yellow? What's that?"

"I'll get you a sample."

"Whatever you say, man." He went over and hauled himself up on the sink to look at the top of the old cabinets. "Oh," he said as an afterthought, "is it okay if I stand on this?"

"Be my guest," I said.

"It's pretty dusty up here."

"Yeah, I don't clean very well."

He seemed surprised. "You don't like to clean?"

"Nobody likes to clean, do they?"

He stuck his thumb in a loop of the tool holder around his waist. "Sorry. I thought maybe you . . . liked to clean."

I looked up at him, his head reaching a few inches from the ceiling. "No, I'm not into cleaning," I said.

"My wife, she cleans all the time."

"Does she?" I said.

"She's real sweet," he said, smearing some dirt on the front of the old cabinet.

"*Is* she?" I said.

"Your friend does the cleaning?" he asked, jumping off the sink.

"We take turns."

"No kidding?"

I noticed that he had tufts of hair on his earlobes. I hadn't noticed those the first day. "No kidding."

"Well, we'd better start emptying the cabinets," I said.

"Do you mind doing that yourself? I have to get some more tools from my truck."

I had started removing some teacups and turned around with one in my hand. "No, I don't mind."

"Those are real cute," he said, gesturing with his head. "Got flowers on 'em, huh?"

"You don't like flowers?" I asked.

"Oh, they're okay. I just don't like 'em too much on cups."

"The cups are pretty tough, flowers and all."

"Is that right?" he said, picking a speck of food out of his back teeth.

"A special glaze. You'd be surprised." I felt like throwing the teacup on the floor to show him, but it might have broken and ruined my point.

"My aunt Maria collects china dishes. She's got all kinds."

"Does she?"

"She's real old now. As long as I can remember she's collected these china dishes. Even back in Cuba."

"Is your aunt gay?" I said.

"Huh?" Then he laughed. "What made you say that?"

"Because she collects china, I guess. That's a sure sign."

He bit his lower lip and cocked his head at me. We both took a beat. I thought his face looked a bit tired, with circles surfacing below the eyes. I suddenly felt his eyes evaluating me, almost picking me up bodily and turning me over.

"I'm afraid I didn't buy any more beer," I said, removing the rest of the teacups from the cabinet.

"You don't have anything to eat by any chance, do you?"

I watched his eyes fall on the rhubarb pie sitting on top of the breadbox. "How about some of this?" I said, lifting it.

"Looks good."

I cut him a big slice and put it on a plate.

"Did you make it yourself?"

I smiled but didn't answer. "Here's a fork," I said, opening a drawer.

"Never mind!" He picked up the piece of pie with his hand and bit into it. Some of the filling oozed out as he took a second bite and then fell on the floor. He didn't seem to notice and I ignored it. "It's delicious!" he said, his mouth full. A couple more swallows and there was nothing left except crumbs on his fingertips. He wiped them on his work pants.

I got some aluminum foil and covered the rest of the pie and put it back on the breadbox.

"You make a real good pie," he said.

"I do my best," I said.

"You've got a sense of humor," he said.

"We always do," I said, taking some glassware out of the cabinet.

I noticed him looking at my ass and turned toward him, pressing my butt into the handle of a drawer. I wondered what he was thinking exactly, although I thought I knew.

I'd caught him staring and he looked embarrassed, but he recovered at once by sticking his thumbs into his belt and hoisting up his pants. "Guess I'd better get that wood from my truck," he said.

"Do I make you nervous?" I said on impulse.

"Me? Why should you make me nervous?"

"Just an idea that crossed my mind."

"No, you seem like a nice guy," he said. Then he coughed, reddening.

"Thanks for the compliment."

"Was that a compliment?" he looked even more embarrassed. "I didn't mean nothing by it."

I bowed. "Thank you."

"I mean—" He began to stumble over his words. "I mean, I don't compliment guys."

"You don't?"

"I mean, I wouldn't know if what I said was a compliment."

"It's all right," I assured him. "No permanent damage done by giving a compliment."

"What do you mean by that?"

I sensed the threat in the way he scowled and clutched the hammer.

"Not a thing," I said, refusing to smile.

It was Fernando who called the following Saturday. "Hey, I'll still fix them cabinets if you want me to," he said. His voice sounded rushed and fretful over the telephone. "I'll give you a special rate because of the delay."

When he came over, he seemed reluctant to get to work and kept coming into the living room, where I was trying to read.

"Yes?" I asked.

"How come I never see your roommate?" he said. He was holding a metal tape-measure and kept pulling out the tape.

"Happened to miss him each time," I said.

"Oh . . ." He hung around the doorway, his arms folded.

"You want to sit down for a minute?"

"Oh, I don't know . . ." He rapped his knuckles on the doorframe.

"Suit yourself." I picked up my book again.

He was still standing there. He'd unbuttoned his plain white shirt since he'd arrived. There was a thicket of hair on his chest, like dry grass.

"Something bothering you?" I said.

He tapped the tape-measure against his thigh. "Oh, I don't know . . ."

"You want to borrow my book, or something?" I held out the novel.

"Don't read too much," he said.

"Men don't," I said.

I watched his eyes take in the plaid drapes and the armchair with the big stuffed frog sitting in it.

"What's the frog for?" he asked.

"For fun. Don't you have one in your house?"

He laughed through his nose. "A frog?"

"No?" I looked at the stuffed frog with the goofy grin on its face. "I was in a play and that was a prop."

"You let it stay in that chair all the time?"

"We move it if we have guests."

"You have a lotta things like that?"

"You mean in the rest of the house?"

"Yeah . . ."

I knew he'd already seen most of the house. "You mean in my bedroom?"

"Wherever . . ."

"What do you have in *your* bedroom?" I countered.

"My wife most of the time!" he snorted.

"Bragging or complaining?" I said.

"She's got big tits."

I didn't say anything.

"You like big tits?"

"I can take 'em or leave 'em."

"See these hands?" He held them out. "These hands shouldn't be working so much. These hands should be full of tits all the time." He pantomimed grabbing handfuls of flesh. It dawned on me that he'd been drinking.

I wondered how it felt to be able to brag about your sex drive like that, never for a moment worrying about what the other man would think.

I crossed my legs and let the book dangle over my knee. "You're quite the stud, aren't you?" I said, almost smiling.

"No complaints yet!"

"If it moves, you'll fuck it, is that it?"

"All it's got to do is lie there," he grinned. "Don't have to move."

I smiled, or at least he thought I did. "Yes, I know the type."

"You didn't offer me any beer or pie this time," he said, resting his elbow on the doorframe.

"Didn't I? I must be forgetting my manners. By the way, you never told me if your wife likes to cook. I bet she does, doesn't she?" I said.

"Yeah, man, she does."

"A real little woman, huh?"

He sensed my irony and dropped his elbow to his side. "I like women to act like women," he said.

"And men to act like men, right?"

"That's right."

"And what does that mean exactly?"

"Huh?"

"Describe being a man to me."

He looked suspicious.

"Go ahead. I'm interested."

He was obviously uncomfortable being asked to speak, but he thought for a moment. "A man is boss and they know their own mind."

"Very interesting. Go on."

He seemed to thrive under the encouragement. "And a man doesn't take no shit from nobody, and he fights when he has to. Like when I was in the Army."

"Sounds admirable."

"And if he acts right, he gets treated like a man." He paused. "Me, I've always been treated like a man."

"And if he acts wrong, what happens to him?" I asked.

But Fernando didn't answer.

We went into the bedroom and I sat on the bed. Fernando stood against the wall.

"You want to remove your shoes at least?" I asked.

He began untying the laces, then put his brown work boots near the clothes rack. After a moment I removed my pants and dropped them on the floor.

"Have you done this before?" I said.

"I used to do it to my cousin, about ten years ago."

I looked at my own belly, glad that the skin looked tight. The exercises seemed to be paying off. I was almost forty myself.

Fernando touched his belt buckle, but the fingers didn't move. He looked ready to run out of the room.

"Changing your mind?" I asked.

He shook his head and undid the buckle. He took off all his clothes. The cock was substantial, but not pornographic. The whole lower part of his body looked very white compared with the tanned top.

I looked at his face, which seemed troubled. There was a ridge where his dark eyebrows came together. He was a forty-year-old man, or close to it, lean and hard and frightened.

"Don't be nervous," I said. I held out my hand.

He finally came over and sat on the edge of the bed next to me.

I put my hand on his leg. He seemed full of tension, almost like electricity. "I think I know what you need," I said. I slid my hand between his legs, down to his ass, and massaged. He tensed. "A guy who gets fucked isn't a real man," he said sadly.

"It's up to you," I said.

"I'm afraid," he whispered. "There's no going back once it's . . ."

I put my arm around his shoulder and hugged him. I felt sorry for him, for all straight men. What a burden they carry. All their violence, all the wars they've killed each other in. "Maybe it's a victory, not a defeat," I said.

As he let me stroke his face, I noticed that his eyes were like a meadow full of ragged flowers. "Are you all right?" I asked.

After a pause he nodded very slowly and lay back on his stomach. I looked at the cleft between the buttocks and ran my hand over the gentle, fuzzy slopes.

"You're sure?" I asked him.

His head nodded on the blanket.

I got a lubricant from the dresser and eased some into the cleft, working my finger down until I touched the tight muscle. It felt more like a bolt than flesh.

I kept my finger on the spot and kissed the underside of his ass near the leg and kept moving my finger back and forth over the muscle, like silk over steel. "Relax . . ." I whispered.

He sighed and raised up, and the bolt loosened a tiny bit.

"Don't be afraid," I said softly.

I put some lubricant on myself and knelt over Fernando, and then placed the tip of my cock at the opening and spread the cheeks. "Is it all right?" I asked. I held my breath. "Is it?" Slowly I entered him with all the tenderness I was capable of.

After several moments he opened like a beautiful, wet flower. "Oh, yes, yes, yes . . ." he sighed.

"Welcome to the other side," I said.

Credit: John Rowberry

Daniel Curzon grew up in Detroit, and attended the University of
Detroit, Kent State University and Wayne State University. He has
taught in his alma maters as well as in the London and Far East
divisions of the University of Maryland and in California State
University at Fresno. He has published four novels: *Something
You Do in the Dark*, *The Misadventures of Tim McPick*, *Among
the Carnivores* and *From Violent Men*. His short stories were
first collected in *Revolt of the Perverts*, several of his plays have
been performed in San Francisco, and he regularly reviews for
the *Los Angeles Times*, *San Francisco Bay Guardian*, *Bay Area
Reporter*, and *San Francisco Sentinel*.

Other Grey Fox Books

Allen Ginsberg   *Composed on the Tongue*
Gates of Wrath
Gay Sunshine Interview (with Allen Young)

Howard Griffin   *Conversations with W. H. Auden*

Richard Hall   *Couplings, A Book of Stories*

Frank O'Hara   *Early Writing*
Poems Retrieved
Standing Still and Walking in New York

Michael Rumaker   *A Day and a Night at the Baths*
My First Satyrnalia

Samuel M. Steward   *Chapters from an Autobiography*

Allen Young   *Gays Under the Cuban Revolution*